MW01181343

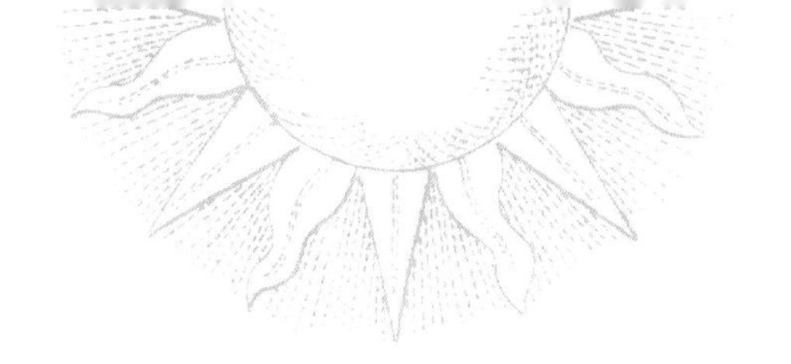

THE GREAT
HISPANIC HERITAGE

Tito Puente

THE GREAT HISPANIC HERITAGE

Isabel Allende

Jorge Luis Borges

Miguel de Cervantes

César Chávez

Roberto Clemente

Salvador Dali

Francisco Goya

Oscar De La Hoya

Dolores Huerta

Frida Kahlo

Jennifer Lopez

Gabriel García Márquez

José Martí

Pedro Martinez

Ellen Ochoa

Pablo Picasso

Tito Puente

Juan Ponce de León

Diego Rivera

Carlos Santana

Sammy Sosa

Pancho Villa

THE GREAT
HISPANIC HERITAGE

Tito Puente

Tim McNeese

Tito Puente

Chelsea House
An imprint of Infobase Publishing
132 West 31st Street
New York NY 10001

Library of Congress Cataloging-in-Publication Data

McNeese, Tim.
Tito Puente / Tim McNeese.
p. cm. — (The great Hispanic heritage series)
Includes bibliographical references and index.
ISBN 978-0-7910-9666-6 (hardcover)
1. Puente, Tito, 1923-2000—Juvenile literature. 2. Salsa musicians—United States—Biography—Juvenile literature. I. Title. II. Series.
ML3930.P83M36 2008
784.4'81888092—dc22
[B] 2007031984

Chelsea House books are available at special discounts when purchased in bulk quantities for businesses, associations, institutions, or sales promotions. Please call our Special Sales Department in New York at (212) 967-8800 or (800) 322-8755.

You can find Chelsea House on the World Wide Web at http://www.chelseahouse.com

Text Design by Takeshi Takahashi
Cover design by Keith Trego and Jooyoung An

Printed in the United States of America

Bang EJB 10 9 8 7 6 5 4 3 2 1

This book is printed on acid-free paper.

Contents

	Introduction	6
1	Finding His Music	16
2	The Young Musician	29
3	To War and Back Again	39
4	The Palladium	53
5	Puente, the 1950s, and Mambo	66
6	Puente's Time and Place	79
7	The Music Continues	92
	Chronology	105
	Notes	108
	Bibliography	110
	Further Reading	111
	Index	113

Introduction

The year was 1940, and the world was on fire. For many Americans, however, the events they read about in their newspapers and magazines, heard about on their radios, and visualized through the newsreels at their local movie houses seemed so distant and unreal. Over the previous two years, Europe had become engulfed by the flames of war. Germany's fascist dictator, Adolf Hitler, had ordered his armies to invade countries that bordered his own, including Austria, Czechoslovakia, and Poland. Once his tanks, bomber planes, armored personnel carriers, motorcycles, artillery units, and masses of men crossed into Polish territory in September 1939, the war became a conflict of epic proportions.

DRUM BEATS OF WAR

Hitler's troops were unstoppable. During the following spring, in a mere matter of weeks, Nazi troops had moved in and occupied five European nations. In a dazzling display of mobility, speed, and crushing might, the Nazis conquered Denmark, Norway, Lichtenstein, Holland, and Belgium. In June 1940, the Germans rolled across yet another international border and brought about the immediate surrender of France. Only Great Britain stood between Hitler and control of Central and Western Europe.

Through the remainder of the summer and into fall 1940, the Nazis invaded Britain from the air. For weeks, German warplanes darkened the skies over the English Channel, dropping endless numbers of bombs on London, England's capital. Fires broke out in the city following each attack, but the people of London held on. Yet, for how long could they hold up under the German assault? Across the Atlantic Ocean, Americans received news of these events as they listened to their radios and the reports delivered by an American reporter in London, a journalist named Edward R. Murrow. Murrow spoke of the attacks and the terrible loss of life.

In the United States, though, the war remained a very distant conflict. After all, Americans were facing their own troubled times. Even as the war was far away, the effects of an economic depression were still present across the American landscape. For a solid decade, the United States had struggled through the worst economic downturn in its history. Many Americans had gone without jobs for years. Husbands and wives had suffered the anguish of failing to provide food for their children. Factories, mines, and scores of other production systems had simply closed their doors, taking away the one thing that gave Americans their dignity—jobs and work. In the United States, the fight was against poverty and economic losses.

Yet, those same radios that broadcast the news of foreign war also delivered what many Americans relied on to help them through such tough times. America's radios provided some relief from reality, and Americans became accustomed to listening to broadcasts that amused and entertained. The programming included serial adventures, dramas, and

The Great Depression was a worldwide economic plunge that lasted through the 1930s. Hundreds of thousands of Americans lost their jobs as small businesses, heavy industry, and farming suffered terrible effects. Shown here are hundreds of jobless New Yorkers waiting in line to get a free dinner at a city lodging house.

comedies. Programs such as *The Bob Hope Show, The Jack Benny Program, The Fred Allen Show, The Lone Ranger, Tarzan, The Green Hornet, Amos and Andy, Blondie,* and cowboy Gene Autry's *Melody Ranch* entertained the American people. Perhaps, most importantly, radio delivered something else that helped Americans the most: music. To many, it was the music that helped them forget the lingering effects of the Great Depression and provided Americans with a break from war reports and the advance of Nazism.

MUSIC IN NEW YORK

Much of the music that Americans listened to in 1940 was broadcast from the country's most important capital of entertainment, New York City. It was the city of the Big Bands, of music groups ranging from soloists to choruses. It was home to so many sounds, not the least of which was a music that had grown to an immense level of popularity and was still growing: Latin music. Latin music made Americans want to get up and dance. It was lively, driven by frenetic beats and tempos. This was music hammered out by Latin artists, many of whom had immigrated to the United States during the 1920s and 1930s from such exotic Caribbean hotspots as Cuba and Puerto Rico.

Latin music could be heard in New York's supper clubs and dance halls. It was played in restaurants and bars. In the city's Spanish Harlem neighborhood, where many of the new Latin-American immigrants lived, some of the most important and popular Latin bands performed. These included Noro Morales, Tito Rodriguez, Xavier Cugat, and Frank Grillo. These were the musicians who were driving Latin music at the opening of the 1940s. They packed music halls, nightclubs, and dance auditoriums with huge crowds made up mostly of young people, Latinos, and African Americans from Harlem, another neighborhood in New York City.

In 1940, a 17-year-old Puerto Rican kid from New York City named Tito Puente was already on his way to becoming the next big thing in Latin music. As a toddler, he had banged on his family's pots and pans, drumming out a youthful, innocent beat. Music was his gift, and it was a gift he had honed for years. By age 15, Tito had been studying piano and drums for half of his life. Puente was already known as El Niño Prodigo, or the Child Prodigy. Music came to him so easily, so intuitively. His curiosity about music, an inherently inquisitive nature, was unquenchable.

In his home neighborhood, El Barrio, he played with his buddies at dances and parties at the local Catholic church and on street corners. Here, the music came naturally and without pretense or formality. It rose from an inborn rhythm found when a talented youth put an instrument in his hands and felt the music as he played it. The teenaged Puente was a regular at the Park Plaza on 110th Street and Fifth Avenue, where he played drums on Sunday afternoon with Federico Pagani's Happy Boys. Puente and the Boys could play it all, including swing, pop, jazz, and Afro-Cuban. But 110th and Fifth was only a street corner. It was, at best, an opportunity waiting to happen. It was while playing with the Happy Boys that Puente took up the instrument that would change his future, the timbales. The timbales are a set of two single-headed, tunable metal drums mounted on a stand and played with sticks and the fingers of the left hand. When those hands and sticks were Tito Puente's, the music flowed, and everyone danced. From Pagani's Happy Boys, Tito landed his next gig at age 16, one that actually paid. It was playing with the Noro Morales Orchestra at the Stork Club. The young Latin kid from El Barrio seemed to be on his way up.

New York was so far away from the haunting violence of the battlefield. Yet, the war was still out there, over the horizons spanned by the Atlantic and Pacific Oceans. The war raged not only in Europe but in Asia as well, where aggressive Japanese warlords had sent their forces against

During the 1930s and 1940s, radio was king in the United States, providing most Americans with their main source of news and entertainment. President Franklin Delano Roosevelt frequently addressed the nation. He spoke about such important issues as the economy and the progress of World War II.

neighboring Asian nations. Their battle cry was to throw out the influence of European colonial powers. "Asia for Asians," is what they claimed. Yet, as Japanese armies moved ruthlessly against Manchuria, Korea, and China, the meaning of the Japanese phrase became clearer. In reality, it was "Asia for Japan."

THE FIGHT COMES TO AMERICA

By 1941, the war had moved against new nations. In the summer of that year, the Germans crossed the border into the vast Soviet Union, beginning a military campaign that would have an impact in every corner of Europe and beyond. The year also brought new opportunities for the teenaged Tito Puente who was asked by Mario Bauza to take a seat with Machito and his orchestra, the Afro-Cubans. The band had big shows to play at two popular New York clubs, La Conga and the Havana-Madrid. Machito's drummer, Cohito, could not read music, and young Tito could. "Get the kid," Machito said to Bauza. "He's the one." It was an opportunity that made Tito's mouth water.

Machito showcased the talented young Tito Puente in his band almost immediately, making him a featured soloist. Tito played the timbales at the front of the stage, where he stood in front of the crowd, driving them wild with his energetic beats. Only once had a timbalist been front and center. That was in 1936 when bandleader Xavier Cugat had put Mano Lopez out front for the opening musical segment of a show called *Go West, Young Man.* With Machito, Tito was going places. Late in 1941, Machito and his Afro-Cuban Orchestra started making recordings for Decca Records. Tito saw new opportunities for himself. This could be the next big break in his climb up the ladder of fame in the world of Latin music. Unfortunately, the band completed only half of the album's songs before worldwide events caught up with the New York music scene. Suddenly, the U.S. government placed a ban on all recordings. There was a war looming out there, and America's resources had to be shifted to wartime needs. Just as fame was finding 18-year-old Tito Puente, the war caught up with him as well.

Japan's surprise attack on the U.S. Fleet at Pearl Harbor on December 7, 1941, marked America's entrance into World War II. The attack destroyed or damaged 18 U.S. ships, including the destroyer USS *Shaw*, shown here as it explodes into flames after being hit by Japanese bombs. *Shaw* was repaired and returned to service several months later.

Then, the war hit full force, changing the rise of the Latin prodigy. On December 7, 1941, hundreds of Japanese fighter planes streaked through the skies over the American territory of the Hawaiian Islands, concentrating on Pearl Harbor. There, dozens of the nation's naval vessels, including eight crucial battleships, were docked. As the Japanese planes approached, they used the song "Sweet Leilani," sung by American crooner Bing Crosby, then being broadcast on Honolulu's radio station, as a radio signal to direct their air attack. Before the early morning assault was over, 18 U.S. ships and 188 planes had been destroyed or damaged and nearly 2,500 American military personnel were killed, wounded, or dying. Eleven-hundred of those had gone down when the battleship *Arizona* had exploded and sunk in the harbor. The war had found America and interrupted the music.

Although the attack had started just after 8:00 A.M. Hawaii time, it was 2:00 P.M. in New York City. At that time, the New York Giants and the Brooklyn Dodgers were playing football. The game was interrupted on WOR radio by the announcement of the Japanese attack at Pearl Harbor. Just before 3:00 P.M., a performance of the New York Philharmonic was stopped to inform the audience of the invasion. At New York's WQXR, radio station officials switched an afternoon broadcast of Gilbert and Sullivan's operetta *The Mikado* to *H.M.S. Pinafore*, as a gesture in support of the British Royal Navy. (*H.M.S. Pinafore*, also written by Gilbert and Sullivan is set against the backdrop of the British Navy.) Indeed, the war was interrupting the music.

Tito Puente heard the news of the attack on his own radio and could only wonder what the future might be for his country. One of his first thoughts had been, *Where the heck is Pearl Harbor?* Then, the realities of war began to sink in, and his response became more personal and profound. "Man, I'm only eighteen!" he exclaimed. That evening, at the Copacabana nightclub, one of the hottest spots for Latin music in New York, uniformed servicemen gathered in large numbers. They also crowded into Times Square and other nightclubs and restaurants, and over on Broadway, and up in Harlem. They were looking for one last drink, and they were searching for a partner for one last dance.

The war had finally reached America. The nation's young men and some of its women would answer the call to duty and leave their old worlds behind to fight a war. Budding music career or not, Tito Puente knew he had to either join the military soon or the army would find him and draft him later. He gave up his timbales and took up duty in the navy. His first assignment would be aboard a small aircraft carrier. By early 1942, Puente was leaving his music behind. What would his future become? Where would the war take him? What about his music career? He had been on his way to the top, and the career that might have been seemed lost forever. Already, the war seemed to have cost him so much, even as the naval vessel that was now his home sailed out into the unknown waters of the future.

1 Finding His Music

Tito Puente was born in New York City, and he died in New York City, yet he would live his life in honor of his Puerto Rican heritage. His parents had migrated to the United States from the Caribbean island of Puerto Rico, which had become an American territory following the Spanish-American War in 1898. His parents, Ernesto and Ercelia Puente, had left Puerto Rico to find new opportunities for themselves and their future children. When they arrived, they immediately looked for a place to live and a job for Ernesto. In time, the elder Puente began working at the Gem razor blade factory in Brooklyn, where he and Ercelia had an apartment. After a few months, they moved to Manhattan's East 110th Street. Ernesto kept working at the Gem factory, riding the subway to his job each morning. He was such a dedicated and competent worker that he was promoted to factory foreman.

Things began to fall into place for the Puentes. They had a new life in America, steady work, and they lived in a neighborhood where they were comfortable and among friends. Soon, the couple started a family. Ernest Anthony Puente was born on April 20, 1923, at the Harlem Hospital. His parents called him "Ernestito."

GROWING UP IN EL BARRIO

Ernestito's neighborhood was a long-established Puerto Rican community in East Harlem that was commonly referred to as Spanish Harlem. It was also known as El Barrio. The family home address was 1850 Madison Avenue. As an adult, Puente remembered how his parents "were one of the first pioneers coming [to the United States] from Puerto Rico, to Atlanta, then Brooklyn. I was born in New York."[1] Yet, Puente's youth was not spent entirely in New York City or even in the United States. When he was one year old, the family went back to Puerto Rico and remained on the island until young Puente was three years old. There, while raising their infant son, the Puentes were able to receive help from family members. Eventually, the United States would become Ernestito's permanent home.

Young Ernest would soon be called "Tito" by his family, the name that would stick throughout his adult life. He would not be the only child of the Puentes. His sister, Anna, was born five years later, and a brother, Robert Anthony, was born in 1929. Robert, however, died tragically when he fell off a fire escape at the age of four. The late 1920s and early 1930s were difficult years for the Puentes. In 1929, the collapse of the stock market and the American economy in general threw the country into the Great Depression. The Depression dragged on for more than a decade. Years later, Puente recalled, "We were very poor. My family used to move . . . a lot to different buildings, you know. Sometimes I'd come from school and I'd find out that they had moved across the street because they gave them two months' rent."[2]

The world in which young Tito was raised might have been poor economically, but it was rich culturally. Puerto Ricans had made their way to the United States even before the annexation of their island home by the United States at the end of the nineteenth century. Some arrived as early as the mid-1800s. They came in small numbers to the United States as late as World War I (1914–1918) because the U.S. government did not recognize them as American citizens. When they gained the right to U.S. citizenship in 1917, the pattern of Puerto Rican migration changed dramatically. Seeing the United States as a land of unique opportunities, many Puerto Ricans could not wait to reach America and start new lives for themselves. No one knows how many Puerto Ricans arrived in America during the decades immediately following World War I because the U.S. Census did not include Puerto Ricans who had U.S. citizenship as foreign-born individuals. Thus, they were simply counted as part of the general American population. The estimates of the number of Puerto Ricans in the States by 1930 range from 45,000 to 100,000.

Many Puerto Rican immigrants settled in a handful of America's major cities but none more than New York City. During the 1920s, the vast majority of Puerto Ricans who reached New York established themselves in five specific neighborhoods, centered in the boroughs of Manhattan and Brooklyn. Spanish Harlem was located on the northern half of Manhattan Island. Many Puerto Ricans lived near waterfront districts. They took dock work and factory jobs. A significant number of them worked in cigar workshops. Yet, even as many New York Puerto Ricans managed to congregate in neighborhoods near one another, there was really no such thing as a neighborhood made up only of Puerto Ricans—or any other ethnic group, for that matter. New York between the wars was home to a wide variety of races and ethnicities where Puerto Ricans rubbed shoulders with everyone from Jews to Germans to Irish to African Americans. The newly arrived Latinos lived in "scattered pockets among a constellation of ethnic groups."[3]

A MULTICULTURAL WORLD

Such mixed neighborhoods were often working-class people who were employed at similar types of labor, who lived close to their workplaces, and who were able to afford the same quality

MAKING THEIR WAY TO AMERICA

The story of how the Puente family came to the United States is a story similar to millions of other families who immigrated to the States in search of a better life for themselves and their descendants. In 1898, the United States and Spain fought the Spanish-America War, in part, over Cuban independence. Spain had held Cuba as a colony for nearly 400 years, and when Cuban revolutionaries rose up in the 1890s to throw off Spanish control, the United States intervened on their behalf. Following the war, Spain gave Cuba and Puerto Rico to the United States. In 1917, the U.S. Congress passed a controversial measure, the Jones Act, which granted Puerto Ricans American citizenship, making them subject to service in the U.S. military.

Following World War I (1914–1918), thousands of Puerto Ricans took advantage of their newly granted American citizenship and migrated to the United States. In spring 1920, 40-year-old Antonio Puente arrived in New York onboard the SS *Coamo*, a British ship. His 16-year-old son, Ernesto, was with him. The father and son took residence at 111 West 134th Street, in New York's El Barrio, or Spanish Harlem.

The Puente men struggled to make ends meet during the early 1920s. Yet, they did find some of the opportunities they had sought by immigrating to the great American city of New York. In the meantime, a young Puerto Rican woman named Ercelia Ortiz, a native of the town of Ponce, made the decision to immigrate to New York as well. She had only been able to work as a housekeeper in her homeland. By 1922, Ernesto Puente and Ercelia Ortiz had found one another, had begun to date, and decided to marry. On Friday, April 20, 1923, they had their first child, Ernest Anthony "Tito" Puente.

of housing. Thus, the Puentes lived among those Puerto Rican immigrants who "carried on daily interethnic negotiations with these people among whom they work and lived, often within the intimacy of boarding arrangements."[4]

In an interview, Puente remembered the diversity of his neighborhood and the difficulties of being Latin American, with its different kinds of foods, customs, and music:

> Well, we did have a lot of barriers, you know, because the neighborhood wasn't really a Spanish neighborhood. A lot of Jewish people used to live there at that time. . . . Around the neighborhood, one side we had the Italians, the other side we had the blacks, and the Puerto Ricans were smack in the middle! One of those things we had a lot of difficulties in getting was our music across, particularly. So we had to incorporate our music within the neighborhood, all the neighborhood clubs—all the Latin music was played there. . . . We were all very close neighborhood Latins there. Puerto Ricans particularly, anyway, and as the years went by, naturally a lot of Cubans and Dominicans, and all kinds of people.[5]

Even in the midst of this diverse world, the Puentes still tried to retain as much of their Puerto Rican culture as possible. Puente later remembered:

> When I was growing up, my parents insisted that we speak Spanish and read Spanish. I'm so happy that they did that, because we developed their culture and their roots. I learned the cultures of the Latin people, which is very important, because in [the United States] at the time that I was being brought up, there was nothing that they taught us about [Latin] culture. America-only history you learn; but Latin American cultures are very big, and I'm very glad that my mother brought me up that way.[6]

Tito was raised in the midst of a thriving community of Latinos that included Puerto Ricans as well as residents from other Latin-American countries. However, even as young Tito was raised to retain as many aspects of his Latin-American heritage as possible, he knew that the English language was an essential part of his upbringing. "I never had any difficulties really," noted Puente in a later interview, "because I spoke English, naturally—since I was born here—and Spanish. So today that's a big advantage to me, being bilingual."[7]

Music came into young Tito Puente's life early. Even as a toddler, "he began to use forks and spoons to bang on the furniture and window sills of their Spanish Harlem apartment."[8] While other parents might have tried to stifle that youthful racket, especially in an apartment with thin walls and neighbors who lived so closely, the Puentes encouraged their young son's affinity for banging around. "I was a very percussive young man," recalled Tito later in life, "always playing on things. My neighbors complained to my parents, 'Why don't you put that brat to study music? He's driving us crazy here!'"[9]

When young Tito was old enough to start elementary school, he attended Public Schools 43 and 184. Then, he went on to Cooper Junior High School and Galvanni Junior High School. Following those, he attended Central Commercial High School. His parents wanted the best for him, and that meant guiding him to those activities that would help the young man make a success of himself.

Music seemed to be a means to that end. Tito's mother was one of the first to recognize the opportunities that music might hold for her children, and she encouraged both Tito and his younger sister, Anna, to participate in neighborhood music and dance groups. When Tito was only 12 years old, he and Anna joined a group known as the Stars of the Future, a local organization that practiced under the tutelage of a neighborhood funeral parlor director. The music group's meetings were

Ernest "Tito" Anthony Puente grew up in New York City, the son of Puerto Rican immigrants, Ernesto and Ercelia Puente. For more than 50 years, Tito entertained audiences with his dance-oriented mambo and Latin jazz works. The King of Latin Music is shown here in the early 1950s.

held at La Milagrosa Catholic Church, located at the corner of 115th Street and Lenox Avenue. This was the neighborhood parish church for the Puente family, "where Tito made his first communion and confirmation."[10]

In fact, the church did more than simply provide a place for the Stars of the Future to meet and make music. Every year, the church held a coronation of the parish's "most talented children who were crowned king and queen for their artistic ability and popularity."[11] During the years of his performing with the Stars, Tito won the king title four times because of his dancing abilities. In his 1935 performance, he was dressed in a blue soldier's cap and uniform, as shown in an existing family photograph. Next to him in the photo are Anna and a friend, Olga San Juan. (Olga would one day become a famous Latin-American movie actress.)

As an adult, Tito Puente would fondly recall these days of practicing and performing music and dancing with his sister. These experiences provided a foundation for his later musical career. In an interview, he remembered the variety of dances he and Anna performed: "Annie and I studied all forms of ball room dancing, including acrobatic tap. We were inspired of course by Fred Astaire and Ginger Rogers. I pride myself on being one of the few bandleaders who really know how to dance. It's something that more young band leaders should investigate."[12]

NEW OPPORTUNITIES

In the music world of El Barrio, Tito Puente's mother found many opportunities for her young son. When a music professor moved into a room Tito's parents rented out to him, he was soon hired to give young Puente alto saxophone lessons. She enrolled him at the New York School of Music on 125th Street and Lenox Avenue, which was close to the family home. Tito later remembered that the lessons cost 25 cents each (not cheap for the time). To provide the quarter for the lessons, Ercelia Puente "would take the quarter from [Tito's] father while he was asleep."[13]

These lessons would prove invaluable in helping to groom the young musician. He took the lessons for seven years, learning to play the piano from Victoria Hernandez, the sister of the most notable Puerto Rican composer of his day, Rafael Hernandez. He also studied piano under Luis Varona, who would later perform as pianist for the Machito Orchestra (which Tito would later join) as well as for Tito Puente's own orchestra. Perhaps just as important to the budding musical artist was Puente's drums instructor, a music teacher and show drummer

BEING HISPANIC

LATINO PRIDE

Musicians often find their identity in their music, and Tito Puente is certainly no exception. Yet, Puente's identity was more than just writing, arranging, and performing Latin music. His music was a special combination of rhythms, beats, sounds, and lyrics that often reflected not only his virtuosity but his ethnic identity. Tito Puente's music was as much about his being Hispanic as it was about him being a professional performer.

In many ways, Tito Puente's Hispanic heritage determined his musical career more than almost any other influence. He was a Puerto Rican, even if his father and mother immigrated to the United States during the 1920s. Tito himself was born in New York City, in the Harlem Hospital, making him a U.S. citizen. He, like so many thousands of Puerto Ricans in New York in the pre-World War II years would speak of themselves as *New Yoricans*. Yet, American citizenship and his physical separation from Puerto Rico did not eliminate the cultural and social influences of his Hispanic roots from Tito Puente's life. His world was a combination of living in America, even as he helped establish Latin music to American audiences.

His timing could not have been better. By the time Puente reached adulthood, New York City was home to much of the popular music of the era. New York in the 1940s was where the Big Band sound established its roots. Other music styles, including early black-generated jazz, were also making their way into America's musical tastes, coming out of the city's Harlem neighborhood. As Puente grew up in the Latin neighborhood of Spanish Harlem, he had the opportunity to enjoy all the great

remembered later as "Mr. Williams." His influence on young Puente was significant, even though his instruction was simply stylistic. Puente later recalled, "[Mr. Williams] knew absolutely nothing about Latin music, but I wasn't going to him for that. He gave me a good foundation; snare drum technique, how to interpret figures in charts and accompany shows."[14]

sounds of his time—swing orchestras, black jazz, and the rhythms of his own ethnicity—Latin music. The Latin music had migrated to New York City during the 1920s and 1930s from such hotspots such as Cuba and Puerto Rico.

Surrounded by all these musical sounds, Tito Puente might have become, as an adult musician, no more than just another performer in another swing band. He might have taken jazz as his own and made a career playing the music founded by another race. Yet, Puente chose instead to take Latin music as his own and change it into his own style utilizing both swing and jazz. The result was a sound that was still so closely associated with Latin rhythms that it brought on a new level of interest in such music, not only among his fellow Latinos, but among blacks and whites as well. Even when Tito Puente took his music out of Spanish Harlem's El Barrio, he was only widening the circle of influence for Latin music.

Through all this, Tito Puente remained a Latino who performed the music of his ethnic heritage. He never abandoned his love of Latin rhythms and dance music that included sambas, rumbas, the cha cha, and other Latin music forms. As a result, the musical heritage of Puente was so closely connected to his ethnicity that the two were inseparable. Tito Puente could not perform his music and leave his ethnicity out of the equation. Throughout most of the twentieth century, he brought new life to Latin music, making him one of the greatest Hispanic performers of his time.

With so much professional influence on young Tito's music, a love of the art was instilled in the developing musician. He had other interests, to be certain. By age 14, he was a member of a local Boy Scout troop that met each week at the American Legion Hall on 5th Street. By 1937, he was attending Central Commercial High School. There, he would begin performing everywhere and at every chance he had. During the school lunch hour, Puente "would be seen in the auditorium with a crowd around him watching him play Boogie Woogie."[15] He put together a group of three or four young musicians and they could be seen performing on a school staircase or after classes on a popular street corner. There, they sang popular songs by the black group the Ink Spots Quartet, including "Sweet Sue" and "Am I Blue."

African-American music had a significant impact on young Tito, and it would remain an influence on him throughout his musical career. He grew up in an urban environment where black families were among his friends, his schoolmates, and his neighbors. Black jazz musicians impacted him as he listened to their music. "Some of them were my mentors," remembered Puente, "like [Duke] Ellington, [Count] Basie at the time, and Lucky Mullinder, and Chick Webb . . . all those bands."[16] Tito listened to lots of jazz music, but he also listened to an abundance of Latin music. It was, after all, the primary music of El Barrio. It was a music that many outside Spanish Harlem, even in New York City, were not commonly exposed to during the 1920s and 1930s. "So I'm very happy I got brought up with both cultures," noted an adult Tito, "and we really got along and developed all our music together through all those years."[17]

GETTING AN EDUCATION

Although the various music lessons Tito Puente experienced were important in developing his talent, he found constant inspiration in the performances of professional musicians he heard on the radio, and, occasionally, was able to hear at live

Pianist, bandleader, and composer William "Count" Basic was one of Tito Puente's primary influences during the late 1930s and 1940s. Basie's bands featured many of the greatest jazz and blues singers of the time, including Billie Holiday, Big Joe Turner, and Joe Williams. He also recorded albums with singers Ella Fitzgerald and Frank Sinatra.

performances. The adult Puente recalled how his piano lessons began after he "had been overwhelmed by Cuban pianist Anselmo Sacassas's solo for Casino De La Playa's RCA recording of "Dolor cobarde."[18]

A few months later, after hearing drummer Gene Krupa perform "Sing, Sing, Sing" with Benny Goodman's orchestra, Puente added trap, or snare, drum to his growing repertoire of musical instruments. In his later years, Puente recalled, "I would listen to the great dance bands of the day on the radio, Goodman, Artie Shaw, Duke Ellington, and I'd go to theaters like the Paramount and the Strand to see them perform. My hero was Gene Krupa. I even won a drum contest playing his solo on 'Sing, Sing, Sing,' note for note."[19]

Music had become the driving rhythm of his life while young Tito Puente was still in high school. In 1939, at the age of 16 and still two years away from graduating, Tito made a fateful decision. He would leave school and spend all his effort and talent pursuing a dream. He set his sights on becoming a full-time, professional musician.

2

The Young Musician

By 1939, 16-year-old Tito Puente already had more professional music instruction than most musicians twice his age. Music had already become the mainstay of his teen years, and he had made the decision to make it his life's work. He even dropped out of high school to kick-start his career into motion. Yet, he ran into an immediate problem in his plans to become a professional musician. At age 16, the young Latin-American performer was too young to become a member of the New York musicians' organization, Local 802 Musicians Union. Without a professional organization membership, a professional music career was almost impossible.

FINDING HIS PLACE

Undaunted, Tito managed to get a union membership across the Hudson River, in New Jersey, although he still lived in New York City, residing at 53 East 110th Street. He was moving ahead with his music career, but he would not be doing so alone. While still 16 years old, Tito met another Latin-American musician who was his age. Pablo Rodriguez was a newly arrived immigrant from Puerto Rico who had come to New York City to make his way in the world, certain of the opportunities America had to offer him. At the time, he was living with his brother, Johnny, not far from Tito. Pablo and Tito met at Casita Maria, a Latin teen establishment located on the same block where the two teenagers lived. At the time, they were playing on the same neighborhood baseball team. They would become fast friends and would remain so for many years. Like Tito, Pablo Rodriguez would one day become one of the most famous and influential Latin music performers in the world. He performed under the name "Tito Rodriguez." Between Rodriguez, Puente, and Machito, who would soon enter Tito Puente's life, they would become the "Big Three" of Afro-Cuban jazz by the 1950s.

Despite his youth, Tito soon found his talents in demand. On a December day, while hanging out at the Musicians Union, Tito got a job. He was hired as a drummer for a local Latin band. It was while performing with that music group that Tito met Jose Curbelo, who was also working with the band. Curbelo, a pianist, had recently arrived from Cuba. When he heard Tito perform, he was immediately impressed with the young musician's drumming talent. "I thought I had seen the best drummers in Cuba," Curbelo later stated in an interview. "Until I saw Tito perform."[20] He was so impressed with the young drummer that Curbelo invited Tito to join him for a three-month run at a club in Miami. Tito agreed and he was soon off to Florida. During those three months, the two musicians roomed together, "each paying $5.00 a week for room rental."[21]

Four years older than Tito, Jose Curbelo was destined to become one of the most influential and famous Cuban orchestra leaders of the 1940s. Born in 1919 in Cuba, Curbelo was drawn to music at a very early age. He proved to be a

Pablo "Tito" Rodriguez *(shown with his band, standing behind the timbales)* was born in Santurce, Puerto Rico. He would become one of the most influential makers of Latin music in the world. His older brother, Johnny, a popular composer and bandleader, inspired young Pablo to become a musician.

prodigy on the piano. He attended the Molinas Conservatory and graduated at the age of 15. During his late teen years, Curbelo worked with several Cuban orchestras, including Los Hermanos Lebartard, Gilberto Valdes, and Havana Riverside. He had only been in New York since May when he met Tito Puente. Through the few years that followed his arrival in America, he worked with Latin bands directed by Xavier Cugat, Juancito Sanabria, and Oscar De La Hoya.

Xavier Cugat, born in Barcelona, Spain, was another bandleader who popularized Latin rhythms in America and beyond. In a career that spanned almost 50 years, Cugat's broad smile and danceable Latin beats made him a popular performer in live performances and movies, as well as on radio, television, and countless recordings.

By 1942, Curbelo formed his own band, a nine-piece group that included two trumpets, three saxes, a bass, timbales, drums, and himself on the piano. He also hired Polito Galindez as his lead singer. Curbelo's band remained popular with New York City club audiences through the 1950s.

He became an important recording artist of Latin music by 1946, with Tito Rodriguez providing vocals and Tito Puente performing on the timbales. For all his popularity, however, Curbelo's band broke up in 1959, and he became a booking agent, as well as a real estate agent.

ESTABLISHING A NEW MUSIC

Tito Puente had the good fortune to meet Curbelo at the beginning of the bandmaster's 20-year North American music career. Curbelo proved to be an important mentor for Tito, "both in music and especially in business."[22] When the paths of these two young musicians first crossed in 1939, it provided an opportunity to form a relationship that would help meld the Latin influences of Cuban and Puerto Rican music together. That unique sound would be presented on the New York music scene.

The door was opening not only for Tito Puente's music career but for Latin music in general. By the late 1930s, Latin music, especially Cuban music, "had begun to pervade the dance halls of Spanish Harlem but was spreading throughout the city."[23] Several classy, elegant nightclubs had opened down in the midtown district of Manhattan. These included clubs with names that revealed their Cuban connections, such as La Conga, Casa Cubana, Club Yumuri, and Havana-Madrid. Cuban dance rhythms were driving the Cuban craze in New York, and the leader of the pack was the rumba. The rumba was a Cuban ballroom dance done in two-quarters or four-quarters time and marked by a step-close-step pattern and pronounced hip movements. Its roots in the Big Apple went back to the early 1930s. Like the tango had with a previous generation of New York clubbers, the rumba had been a hit in Harlem, as well as in the white-dominated clubs of midtown.

The rumba may first have received serious attention in New York in spring 1930. Music historians even identify a specific performance at a specific place and date. On Saturday afternoon April 26, the curtain rose for a program at New

York's Palace Theater. The band on stage was Don Azpiazu's Havana Casino Orchestra. It was the band's third song and its performance that delivered a new sound and "the course of both Latin music and jazz in the United States was irrevocably changed."[24] The song was titled "El Manicero," or "The Peanut Vendor."

"The Peanut Vendor" was an uncompromising song that stuck close to its Cuban roots, including the appropriate instrumentation. Don Azpiazu's band presented an accurate Cuban dance sound. They delivered that sound using maracas, claves, bongos, and timbales, the standard and unique instruments in the Cuban rhythmic arsenal. Azpiazu had cut his teeth musically in Cuba where he had become a controversial bandleader at the upscale Havana Casino "by introducing what were regarded as lower-class Cuban pieces into his repertoire there."[25] With this background, Azpiazu hit New York ready to make changes in the city's music scene. "The Peanut Vendor" did just that. It was an authentic piece of Cuban music. Then, when Azpiazu recorded the song with his band in May 1930 for RCA Victor Records, it hit America for a loop. Suddenly, the popular music scene of the 1930s experienced serious "Latinization." Azpiazu is often overlooked as an influence on behalf of Latin music in the United States, but he made his contributions throughout the 1930s. With his rendition of "The Peanut Vendor," Azpiazu proved himself to be an innovator 15 years ahead of his time. Because of him, the early 1930s witnessed a number of New York studio orchestras that added "Havana" to their names.

Others contributed their music to the equation as well. During late summer 1930, a pair of Cuban rumba bands was playing in the Lafayette Theater, which was Harlem's primary vaudeville house. The following summer, the Lafayette hosted "Rhumba-Land," a show led by vocalist Antonio Machín and his Royal Havana Troupe. The revue also featured blues singer Mamie Smith and jazz drummer Kaiser Marshall's band, Czars of Harlem. Later that fall, a new show premiered

Frank "Machito" Grillo was born in Havana, Cuba. His band, the Afro-Cubans, revolutionized Latin music with the introduction of jazz improvisation. Machito was the front man, singer, and conductor of his bands. By the 1950s, Machito, Tito Rodriguez, and Tito Puente were the major creators of Afro-Cuban jazz.

at the Lafayette called "Rhapsody in Black," which, along with singers Ethel Waters and Eddie Rector, included the number "Harlem Rhumbola," sung by Bessie Dudley.

That September, the *New York Amsterdam News* reported "on what sounds like the first piece of Cuban-derived Latin Jazz created in the U.S."[26] It was performed at a show called "Fast and Furious" at Brandt's Theatre, in Jackson Heights, Queens, another borough of New York City. The music was written by Broadway songwriters Mack Gordon and Harry Revel. In the review of the program, the song "Rhumbatism" was referred to as "an outstanding song number . . . a frenzied

MACHITO, ANOTHER GREAT LATIN BANDLEADER

For more than 40 years, Machito was one of the most important musicians to contribute to the sounds of Afro-Cuban jazz. He was born and raised in Cuba. There, he met Mario Bauza, who would one day become the father and founder of Afro-Cuban jazz. Throughout the 1930s, Machito performed in some of Cuba's most popular nightspots. In 1936, Bauza, who had already moved to New York, convinced Machito to join him. Machito arrived in the city in October 1937.

Within a week of his arrival, Machito landed a singing gig. His reputation as a hotshot Cuban jazz vocalist soon spread. Then Machito and Bauza attempted to launch an orchestra in 1939, but their efforts failed. The two found separate work, yet Machito still yearned to lead his own band. In 1940, he formed the Afro-Cubans.

The band was formed originally as a "vocal and ensemble-oriented unit,"* but Machito tweaked his ensemble's sounds. One of those changes came with the addition of Bauza as the group's trumpeter, as well as its key arranger. Bauza also hired soloists with solid jazz backgrounds. One of the band's newest additions was a Latin drummer, then only 17 years old, Tito Puente.

jazz affair. . . . This is something new and worth more play . . . than it is given here."[27] While the song obviously had Latin-American overtones, "Rhumbatism" was sung and danced to by Jackie Mabley, who would later become known as the comedian Moms Mabley. All through the 1930s, Latin music was getting attention, and it was being performed by both Latin and African-American bands.

PUENTE MEETS MACHITO

While young Tito Puente's apprenticeship to Jose Curbelo would help form him further as a musician, Tito would be

Machito was drafted into the military in spring 1943, although the band continued under Bauza's leadership. Before year's end, Machito's military career was cut short by an accident. He wasted no time getting back to New York City where he took up leadership of his band once more.

Upon his return, Machito's career continued to thrive, performing with the leading Big Bands and jazz musicians of the postwar era, including Duke Ellington and Charlie Parker. He was also recording on the Clef label.

Into the 1950s, Machito's band was as popular as ever, performing music that swung from jazz to bebop and Cuban dance numbers. They regularly performed at the Palladium. Ultimately, Machito continued to perform into the 1980s. (Bauza had finally left the band in 1976 after 35 years.) In his mid-sixties, Machito had hired his own son, Mario, to direct the band, and brought in his daughter, Paula, as female vocalist. He was still performing at age 72. He died in London in 1984 after suffering a heart attack.

* Scott Yanow, *Afro-Cuban Jazz* (San Francisco: Miller Freeman Books, 2000), 66.

impacted by his connection with another Latin musician. This was Cuban bandleader Frank Grillo, who was known professionally by the name Machito. He had migrated to the United States in 1937 and would "become Puente's principal musical model."[28] Machito arrived in New York in October and soon found work as a musician at one of New York's Latin clubs, Las Estrellas Habanera.

Tito Puente remembered meeting Machito when he was 13 or 14 years old. Machito performed in El Barrio, which gave the young Tito the opportunity to hear him, as well as play for him. These were days Puente would remember well as an adult:

> I played with him in the neighborhood, during the weekend, because we used to perform on 110th Street and Fifth Avenue near the [Park] Plaza, we used to call it. And I used to come in on Sundays and sit in, and I was still going to school and all that, so naturally we got along, they saw my talents and all that. They really loved me. They loved my parents—you know most of the people in the neighborhood, they all knew each other. So I used to come in and play all the time.[29]

Young Tito would learn many aspects of musicianship and style from Machito and musicians who played with him. Tito learned about the music of the street players who performed around the neighborhood. Having no professional gig to play in a theater, dance hall, or nightclub, such street performers played with one another, informally, sharing styles and instrumentation. Puente recalled the formative value of this and how "it was very important to play, jamming a lot with the Cubans, playing timbales and drums."[30] Under Machito's guidance, Tito played the saxophone and the piano, jamming with the professionals at every opportunity. Eventually, Tito's connection with Machito would move past the learning stage. By 1941, Machito was using the 17-year-old Puente as a drummer in his band.

3

To War and Back Again

The influences of such important musicians as Curbelo and Machito on Tito Puente are incalculable. Yet, the young Puerto Rican would also find his *own* way onto the stage as a professional musician. Just when he met Curbelo, Tito was beginning to play for John Rodriguez's Stork Club Orchestra, and, after that, for Anselmo Sacassas's band at Chicago's Colony Club. By 1941, when Puente turned 18 years old, he was recording albums as the drummer for Vincent Lopez's Swing Orchestra. These recordings included the Latin songs "Los hijos de Buda," "Yumba," "La conga," and "Cachita." His career was taking off, and Tito had no trouble finding more and more work. Before the end of 1941, he also drummed for bandleader Noro Morales.

A POPULAR CUBAN BANDLEADER

Morales was one of the most popular Afro-Cuban bandleaders of the 1940s, rivaling even Machito for a time. Born in 1911, he was the son of a Puerto Rican violinist. Noro began playing music at an early age. In 1924, his father moved the family to Caracas, Venezuela, to take a job as the musical director for the Official Court Orchestra. Sadly, young Morales's father died only a few months after moving to Caracas, and Noro, then only 13 years old, was selected to take his father's place. By 1930, the Morales family moved back to Puerto Rico. Noro remained there for five years, working as a freelance pianist with several Latin bands, including the Midnight Serenaders. In 1935, he left his homeland and moved to New York, where he worked with several Latin bands, such as the Alberto Socarras Orchestra (which Tito Puente would drum for just a few years later), Augusto Coen, and Johnny Rodriguez, Tito Rodriguez's brother. By 1938, he organized the Morales Brothers Orchestra, with his siblings, Humberto on drums and Esy on flute. The band existed only three months, and the name was then changed to the Nino Morales Orchestra. The band was given a five-year stint at the El Morocco nightclub where they became one of New York City's most important Latin groups. It was during this time period that Tito Puente played drums for Morales.

The year 1942 would be an important year of new opportunity for Puente. While working for Morales, Puente appeared in several short films that featured the Morales Orchestra, including *The Gay Ranchero, Ella, Cuban Pete,* and *The Mexican Jumping Bean.* The Morales band was also recording heavily, including albums with Decca Records. Despite the exposure Tito Puente gained with the Morales group, he did not remain with the band even through 1942. That summer, he jumped to another band, replacing Tony Escolies in the Machito Orchestra. With Machito, Puente was still recording albums with Decca, including arrangements of "Oye Negra," (a song that had actually been written by Nino Morales), "El Botellero," and "Eco."

As Tito Puente performed with these bands in the late 1930s and early 1940s, he was beginning to be recognized for his unique drumming style. Foremost among his admirers was Mario Bauza, the music director for Machito's band. It was with Machito that Puente was to be featured as a soloist, "bringing his timbales to the front of the stage where he played standing up rather than seated as had been the approved method until this point."[31] Given his work with the Machito band, as well as earlier opportunities with Jose Curbelo and others, Tito Puente was "proving to be one of the first drummers in Latin music to use a combination of timbales, bass drum, and cymbal to 'kick' big band figures, often without bongo or conga accompaniment."[32] Puente's reputation as a leading Latin music drummer was taking him to new heights. He was a musician in demand. Puente was lured away from Machito to join the Jack Cole Dancers, but he soon returned to the Machito Orchestra. Then, with his star still rising, history stepped in and interrupted Puente's ascent.

IN THE NAVY NOW

Throughout much of the 1930s, the advance of fascist dictators in Europe and of militaristic warlords in Japan had brought on the events that would lead to World War II. By 1939, Europe was at full-scale war, following the German invasion of Poland on September 1. Within two days, Great Britain and France declared war on Hitler, and World War II was on its way to becoming the largest military conflict in the history of the world. Within a week of the Japanese attack on Pearl Harbor, America was not only at war with Japan, but with fascist Italy and Nazi Germany. (Following the attack by Japan, Germany and Italy both declared war on the United States, leading to a reciprocal declaration by the Americans.) War meant a dramatic increase in the number of America's soldiers. By 1942, Tito Puente was among them.

Trumpet player Mario Bauza *(left)*, shown with his brother-in-law, Machito, was born in Havana, Cuba. Bauza and fellow trumpeter Dizzy Gillespie pioneered "Cubop," one of the first types of Latin jazz. Bauza also served as musical director for Machito's Afro-Cubans band from 1941 to 1976. He led his own bands in the 1980s and 1990s.

Many of the young Latin-American men who either joined the military or were drafted into service had moved to the United States between the end of World War I and the beginning of World War II. Those who had come to New York to work as professional musicians were impacted just as much as any other group of Latin immigrants. As a result, many of "the musicians who migrated to New York City in the years between the world wars were born in a transitional era. They were the inheritors of older traditions and practices and the beneficiaries of some new ones."[33] This new generation would go to war for their adopted country and many "Latino soldiers became highly decorated war heroes both in Europe and the South Pacific."[34]

Before and after the war, Latin-American culture would have a dramatic social impact on the country, adding its own contributions in various areas, including music. Hollywood had noticed the increased presence and impact that Latin-American immigrants were having on the culture and had already capitalized on this influence through films, such as the shorts that Tito Puente appeared in earlier. Some Latin Americans were already stars whom many Americans easily recognized, such as Spanish-American actress Rita Hayworth; the performer-actress Carmen Miranda; and the Latin bandleader, Xavier Cugat. The South American tango had already found its way decades earlier to the American dance floor, along with the Cuban rumba, which had been more recently introduced. The mambo was also being incorporated into the sounds of the big swing bands. Such music was even featured in several Hollywood films, even if these forms were commonly used as background themes. While World War II may have interrupted the career paths of several Latin-American performers and musicians, it also helped to further enhance the ultimate effect that Latin culture was going to have on the next generation of Americans.

PUENTE GOES TO WAR

Tito Puente donned a sailor's uniform in 1942 when he was 19 years old. After completing his boot camp experience, Navy officials assigned him to serve on a converted aircraft carrier, the U.S.S. *Santee*. The ship functioned as an escort vessel for supply and passenger ships. Of course, even as Tito had been forced to put his professional music career on hold, he was not about to put his music in mothballs. He gained a place in the ship's band, playing the alto sax. Soon, he and his bandmates were performing for the crew of the *Santee.* Their repertoire included such popular songs and swing band standards as "Sunny Side of the Street," "Green Eyes," "Just Friends," "Sweet Georgia Brown," "How High the Moon," and "One O'Clock Jump." While the band was an important part of Puente's service onboard the *Santee,* he had a military job to perform as well. He was one of the sailors assigned to load ammunition into the ship's artillery pieces.

It was through his work with the ship's band that Puente came to know one of the *Santee*'s pilots, a lieutenant who had played for the Charlie Spivak Orchestra. He was not only a band member who played the tenor saxophone, but he was the band's arranger. Arranging was an aspect of music that Puente had done little of, and his association with a former member of Spivak's orchestra gave him valuable experience writing music. In Puente's words: "[He] showed me the foundation of writing a good chart, how to lay out voicing and get colors out of the brass and reeds. I began writing [music] at this time."[35] Under the tutelage of his lieutenant pal, Puente wrote an arrangement of "El Bajo de Chapotin," which he sent to Machito. Soon, Machito's band was performing Puente's arrangement.

Such opportunities were important for Puente and his otherwise stalled career. As he later remembered the experience of trying to maintain connections with his music while onboard an aircraft carrier, Puente noted:

> I learned a lot also while I was in the service besides doing my duties there on the ship. My professional life was at a standstill, but I was still learning, studying. I used to play drums on the ship, and then I went over to saxophone. We used to have five saxophones. I used to play alto, and then I was writing, already scoring for the bands the nice jazz-pop music at

In this photo from the mid-1950s, Tito Puente is shown playing the timbales. A cowbell is mounted on the timbales stand, and a cymbal is to the left. Using a variety of stick shots and hand strokes, a master *timbalero*, such as Tito Puente, can produce an endless range of rhythms and percussive sounds.

> the time; not heavy jazz bebop or anything like that. There I developed a lot of experience in writing. During the service I had time for that.[36]

During Puente's shipboard service, he and his crewmates participated in nine battles in both Atlantic and Pacific waters. There were additional difficulties that Puente faced during his war years. He was at sea when he received tragic news from home about his younger sister. Anna, who had earlier contracted spinal meningitis, died from the disease. Puente was given a weeklong emergency leave to be with his family. While in New York, Puente took his parents to a Puerto Rican night club, La Perla del Sur, located at 116th Street and Madison Avenue. That evening, he performed two piano tribute numbers. One was for his mother, called "Mis Amores," and the second was for his sister, Debussy's "Clair de Lune."

BACK TO HIS MUSIC CAREER

In December 1944, Puente married Milta Sanchez. He remained in service to the U.S. Navy until he was discharged in 1945. For his military activities, the Puerto Rican immigrant won a presidential commendation. Naturally, once he shed his uniform, he went home to New York City to take back his old job with the Machito Orchestra. (A federal law required employers to offer former servicemen their old jobs if they wanted them.) Things were not that simple in reality, however. The musician who had taken Puente's place, a drummer named Uba Nieto, "had a family to support, and both Machito and Tito agreed that it would be better if Nieto kept his position."[37]

Puente was not without a job for long, however. He soon gained a seat on Frank Marti's Copacabana Band. Following that gig, he was a member of Jose Curbelo's orchestra, and then he joined a Brazilian band directed by Fernando Alvarez. In an interview given many years later, Puente recalled those postwar days and how he was driven to be the best musician he could be:

> At that time the Latin bands were playing nightclubs downtown like the Conga and the Havana Madrid. You had to be a good musician because we played the shows too, not just dance music or barrio music like in Spanish Harlem. You had to play waltzes, tangos, sambas, boleros. That's how I developed my experience in reading and playing all types of music. In the studio too, man, you had to know how to read music. You went in and you stopped at the eighth bar and you started on the ninth. Most of the Latin percussion musicians didn't read much music. They always depended on the ear. Your ear can only go so far. Really, you just have to learn your profession, your instrument. This is it. You have to study.[38]

By fall 1947, Puente made another jump as a band member and became the drummer, contractor, and musical director for Pupi Campo's orchestra. Sometimes the Campo band performed on the same circuit as Curbelo's orchestra. (There were times when the two bands shared billing at the Havana Madrid on 58th Street along with singer Dean Martin and slapstick comedian Jerry Lewis. Campo himself sometimes actually joined Martin and Lewis as the comedy team's third member.) The move to Campo's band would be an important and influential one for Puente. It gave him the opportunity to meet trumpeter Jimmy Frisaura. The two performers became fast friends, forming a bond that would continue for the next 40 years. Frisaura would also perform with Tito and serve as contractor for Puente's various bands during those years.

The postwar years were crucial years for Americans in general and for Puente and Latin-American music in the States as well. Millions of U.S. servicemen left the military and returned home to find that America had itself changed. The postwar years would be the beginning of a new era for the country. The Great Depression of the 1930s seemed so long ago, and many tried to put many of their wartime memories behind them. The future looked new, bright, and unclouded. People hoped these years would be as full of possibility and promise as any others in American history. In New York City, life was evolving for many into another existence, especially in the Latin-American communities.

While tens of thousands of Latinos, including large numbers of Puerto Ricans, had immigrated to the States between the wars, even greater numbers migrated to America following World War II. New arrivals to the Big Apple could find themselves in the midst of a welcoming neighborhood of people just like themselves—Latinos who had beaten them to America by a generation. After the war, there was "the continuous exchange between New York and San Juan."[39] The movement was not simply a one-way street for many Puerto Ricans. The movement *between* New York and Puerto Rico was "intensified by cheap commercial flights after World War II, [creating] a migratory circuit between the two cities that [maintained] kinship and friendship ties on both shores."[40]

BACK TO SCHOOL

Upon his return to the city, Puente did not simply slip back into the same old roles he had earlier. He found plenty of work, and he also set a new course for himself, beginning with music school. Having already made a name for himself on the New York music scene, not just any school would do. He set his sights on the Juilliard School of Music, the most prestigious school of its kind in New York, if not the entire country. "What happened was that after the war the government would pay half of your studying fees if you went to study," explained Puente in an interview. "So, first . . . I gave the audition—because you have to take an exam before joining Juilliard."[41] With federal government monies from the G.I. Bill, Puente soon began taking classes at Juilliard.

From 1945 to 1947, Puente studied conducting, orchestration, and theory. Having already developed some basic arranging skills during his World War II days, he took that skill even further. The heart of that study at Juilliard was based on the Schillinger System of Music, which Puente studied under Richard Bender. The music system was "developed by mathematician and theorist Joseph Schillinger [and] a popular method among jazz musicians including Stan Kenton, whose writing influenced Tito greatly."[42] (Schillinger was a Russian academic who also composed extensive theoretical works. He taught at several New York institutions of higher learning, including the New School for Social Research, New York University, and Columbia University.) Schillinger gave Puente the tools he needed to further his ability to arrange and write music scores.

Juilliard offered Tito Puente opportunities that street level musicians could not have. He later recalled the lessons he received at the school and the value of those experiences:

> Those Juilliard lessons were $15, very expensive. I used to pay $7.50 and the GI Bill paid the other $7.50. I was trying to learn how to write motion picture music. Schillinger's graphs and the permutation of melodies interested me, but I found that wasn't my main goal. I stopped studying there a couple of years later and developed my style by performing and playing. Everybody reads the same books. Everybody goes to school. Everybody studies. Everybody graduates and gets a big diploma. They go home and put it up on the wall, and they just stare at it all the time. Musicians, dentists, doctors, everybody, it's the same thing. But to really learn, you've got to go on and practice and gain experience by playing in front of an audience.[43]

During his time at Juilliard, Puente took up a new instrument, the vibraphone, "which was being used considerably by young musicians and which he began to feature on his interpretations of ballads."[44] The vibraphone, or the vibes, is a percussion instrument similar in appearance to the xylophone. The primary difference between the two instruments is that vibraphone players tap on metal bars, rather than the wooden ones found on a xylophone. Hitting the metal bars produces a clearer, sharper sound, compared with the heavier, denser effect of the xylophone. In addition, a vibraphone includes a device that allows the tones to vibrate longer.

Puente's music was pinballing back and forth between his studies at Juilliard and his work with various Latin bands. While playing with Pupi Campo's orchestra, Puente rubbed shoulders with one of the musicians who played piano for Campo. He was Jose Esteves Jr., known by his music-loving fans as Joe Loco. An extremely talented and versatile composer and arranger, Joe Loco had already played for Machito, Noro Morales, and Count Basie. He had studied music at New York University, and he was familiar with the Schillinger system. Joe Loco and Puente collaborated on several songs for the Pupi Campo Band. They also wrote arrangements on their own. When the band cut an album that included one of their arrangements, they made certain that each got the appropriate credit by having his name appear on the disk label as the arranger. Some of Tito Puente's most important arrangements during the late 1940s were "How High the Moon," "Son de la Loma," "Esta Frizao," and "Pierdate." He was also writing songs at this time, including "Pilarena," "Cuando te Vea," and "The Earl Wilson Mambo."

INTO THE RECORDING STUDIO

In 1948, Latin music was in full swing. So was Tito Puente's career. Late that year, he made his first recordings with Tico Records, a company he stayed with for many fruitful years. The Tico label was founded by George Goldner, who was recording several of New York's Latin bands during the 1940s and 1950s.

Puente recorded his album at WOR studios on 48th St. and Seventh Avenue in New York City. Even at this early point in his career, Puente was already trying to be as innovative as he could be. He came to the studio wanting "to try something

"Joe Loco"

Joe Loco is not well remembered today by music enthusiasts, but, by the 1950s, the Joe Loco Trio was an extremely popular Latin group performing Afro-Cuban jazz. He was two years older than Puente, but, just the opposite of Puente, Loco was born in New York and died in Puerto Rico. He began studying music when he was only eight years old, taking dance and violin lessons. He dropped out of school at age 13 to dance on the vaudeville stage, but, by age 16, "a truant officer caught him and he was forced to attend Harlem High School."* His return to school only helped to enhance Loco's future as a musician, for it was there that he learned to play both the trombone and piano. In time, it would be the piano that would become Loco's main instrument.

During the late 1930s, he performed with several bands as a pianist, including Montecino's Happy Boys, Xavier Cugat, and Machito, whom he worked with from 1943 to 1945, when Puente was already serving in the military. By November 1945, Loco was drafted into the U.S. Air Force where he served until 1947. By spring 1947, he began studying at Juilliard, while, like Puente, performing with several different bands, such as Pupi Campo's and Fernando Alvarez's Copacabana Samba Band. (Puente and Loco not only worked with Campo's band but in Alvarez's as well.) Through the late 1940s, Jose Loco worked as an arranger for Tito Rodriguez, Machito, Noro Morales, and Tito Puente, who had his own band by then.

* Scott Yanow, *Afro-Cuban Jazz* (San Francisco: Miller Freeman Books, 2000), 64.

different with the augmented band, which included Mario Bauza and Graciela (Machito's sister)."[45] Musician Frankie Colon, who played congas for the recording session, remembered Puente's approach to the studio experience:

> After recording three other tunes, Tito surprised us by passing out his charts for "Abaniquito," and dismissing the trombones and saxophones. The remaining musicians were Chino Pozo, Varona on piano, the four trumpeters, Frisaura, Di Risi, Gonzalez, and Mario Bauza, vocalists Graciela, Vincentico Valdes, and me. Vincentico was outta-sight ad-libbing and Mario blew his . . . off on the solo.[46]

The musicians blasted and pounded out their version of the newly arranged number that Puente had thrown at them. Following that initial take, Puente and his musicians listened to it. When Tito wanted to do a second recording, "Mario convinced him not to, insisting another take wouldn't come out as fiery."[47]

Tito Puente was well on his way to becoming a star. He was making music, writing songs, getting credit on album labels for arranging, and finding himself at the forefront of the professional music world of the Big Apple and beyond. He was a known, a name in the industry, and a nightclub and dance floor favorite. Yet, even brighter days were ahead for this Latin-American star. They would guide Tito Puente to a new stage on which to perform. During the 1940s, this venue was known as the Alma Dance Studios. By the opening of the next decade, it would be known as the Palladium. It was there that Tito Puente became a music legend.

4

The Palladium

By the late 1940s and through the 1950s, Latin music found a new home, one that would provide a stage for the elaboration and popular development of the music genre. It was the Palladium, a club situated in downtown Manhattan. The club became a scene for such important Latin bands as Machito, Tito Rodriguez, and, by the 1950s, Tito Puente. This Manhattan hotspot, however, was more than simply a magnet for Afro-Cuban jazz. It "became a multicultural forum for what might now be called performance art."[48] Several important elements of Latin music were providing a swirl of change that would alter the world of Tito Puente. Jazz performers were becoming more interested in Latin dances. Mario Bauza was leading the way by blending jazz elements with bop, creating driving new dance beats. Tito Puente would become a major player in this musical shift, and he brought it all together at the Palladium.

A NEW DISCOVERY

It began with a "discovery" at the Embassy Club in New York in summer 1948. A local dance promoter, Federico Pagani, was watching a show at the club featuring the Campo band. Puente was performing in the orchestra. At the end of one of the band's numbers, Pagani watched as Puente turned and spoke with fellow band member Joe Loco, and then played a few bars on the piano. Puente then sang out a melody he wanted duplicated by bassist Manuel Patot (Pacho) and trumpeter Chino Gonzalez. What followed was one of Latin music's rare moments, as the haunting melody raised goose bumps. Pagani said, "The music was so arousing it made my blood turn cold." After the tune ended, Pagani asked Puente for the name of the tune. "I haven't titled it yet," said Puente, "es un peccadillo" (it's a mishmash).[49]

When asked years later about the title, Puente explained, "I was going to give the tune an Oriental title because of the strong Oriental feel of the melody."[50] When Tito recorded his tune the following year, he named it "Picadillo," a clearly non-Asian title. Ironically, when the song was recorded in 1950 by musician Miguelito Valdes, he would title it "Chang."

It was that improvisational performance at the Embassy Club that inspired Pagani to give Puente his own gig, a Sunday matinee dance at the Alma Dance Studios (renamed a year later as the Palladium). Back in the 1940s, the Alma Dance Studios had served as a popular dance academy, where "men could buy tickets and dance with hostesses."[51] The studios had been redone as a nightclub in 1946 by its owner, Tommy Morton. At that time, there were as many as 15 dance academies in New York, but the two most popular were Roseland and the Arcadia. They were the two hotspots, and all the others were considered secondary.

A NEW VENUE FOR LATIN MUSIC

Morton wanted his new Palladium to be a popular music and dance spot, so he hired such bandleaders as Machito and Mario Bauza "because they had such a tremendous following, they were great record sellers."[52] Morton did not bring in these two just for their Latin music. Machito was known as a bandleader whose musicians could play foxtrots and waltzes, as well as boleros and rumbas. When Morton set them up at the Palladium to play for the non-Latin music crowd, however, audiences did not show up. Then, Bauza asked Morton, "How do you feel about black people [a large part of typical Latin music audiences]?" Morton dryly said, "Look, I'm only interested in the color of green [money]." Bauza responded, "Why don't you try Latin dance here? Let me set this up for you and see what you think about it, okay?" Previously, the Latinos in Harlem had rarely left El Barrio to hear their music, never venturing south of 110th Street. Their homes for Latin music were the Savoy or the Park Place Ballroom. When Bauza and Machito finally struck up their Latin beats at the Palladium, Latin music had finally found its way downtown. The Palladium would remain "the home of Latin music and the home of the mambo until it closed in 1966."[53]

Bauza and Machito would not be the only Latin musicians to play the Palladium. Others included Federico Pagani, who had earlier led the Happy Boys. It was Pagani who worked up a scheme to draw Latin fans to the Palladium. He created the Blen Blen Club, named after a popular Latin song, "Blen-Blen-Blen." They would first play at the Palladium on Sundays. To prime the pump and draw its first crowds of Latin enthusiasts, Pagani hawked discount cards in subway stations and bus stops in the Barrio and beyond. When the first Sunday for the Blen Blen Club arrived, a long line formed outside the dance club that afternoon at 4:00 P.M. They were waiting to hear the six bands that had been booked for opening night, including Noro Morales, Jose Curbelo, and, of course, Machito, who was headlining. According to music historian, Max Salazar: "The six Latin bands brought all the Latinos, the blacks, the whites, and the mulattos from Harlem and Brooklyn, [and Morton] made more money on that one Sunday than he had done for the months since he had opened up."[54] As for Roseland and Arcadia, their business was not hurt dramatically. Their audiences were, after all, almost exclusively white.

PUENTE'S INNOVATIVE SOUNDS

As Tito Puente's music career developed, he was also becoming a broader musician through an expanding résumé that included musicianship, showmanship, virtuosity, and innovative compositional talents. He was also busy proving his abilities as a songwriter and arranger. During the period from 1949 through 1951, three of his compositions stand as works that typified the Puente sound, "Picadillo," "Abaniquito," and "Esy."

Puente wrote "Picadillo" in 1948. He had originally referred to the tune as "*un peccadillo,*" or a "mish-mash." Tito achieved an "Oriental" sound on the tune by putting the song "immediately into motion with an opening brass theme following an eight-bar tumbao-patterned solo for bass and piano left hand."*

The instrumental then moves through an arrangement that switches from its main brass opening into a syncopated piano solo. The entire arrangement is spare, "yet it affords both musician and dancer the opportunity to create and embellish in a most expansive palette of possibilities."**

For Puente, much of what he was trying to do with a song like "Picadillo" hinged on the number's rhythmic qualities. As he described himself in an interview: "I am a rhythmic, syncopated arranger mostly. I am involved with rhythmic forms of a percussive type of arranging where I interject a lot of brass with Latin percussion, because in our music, brass is a very

When Puente was hired to play at the Palladium, he did not have his own performing group, so he put together a pickup band. They named themselves Tito Puente and the Picadilly Boys. Most of the group came from the Campo band and included Jimmy Frisaura, Al Di Risi, Tony Di Risi on trumpet, Manuel Patot on bass, Angel Rosa on vocals, Chino Pozo on bongos, and a number of pianists including Al Escobar, Luis Varona, and Charlie Palmieri. Puente took

essential instrument due to the fact that many years ago in Cuba some of the *conjuntos*, like in Mexico, were always using trumpets.[***]

Puente's first major hit as a bandleader and songwriter and arranger was his "Albanquito," recorded in 1949. The song's opening line relies on a bass and piano, which is followed by a repetitious brass riff, supported by bongo improvisations. The vocals are simple, improvised lines, which are echoed by a repeated chorus.

The third Puente standard from that period was an instrumental mambo, "Esy," recorded in 1951. "Esy" was different from "Picadillo," including "its general style, voicing, orchestration, and melodic rhythm."[†] Among its most intriguing features is a piano opening that slides into a trumpet variation followed by a saxophone line. The song typified Puente's attempts at writing a piece that further integrated Latin music with jazz. With this number, Puente was creating a new approach to Latin dance.

* Steven Loza, *Tito Puente and the Making of Latin Music* (Urbana, Ill: University of Illinois Press, 1999), 27.

** Ibid.

*** Tito Puente, Recorded Lecture, University of California, Los Angeles, May, 1984.

† Loza, 135.

his place at the head of the band, playing his trademark timbales and vibes.

LEADING HIS OWN BAND

It was the beginning of Tito Puente as a bandleader on his own. The band's reputation spread quickly with club audiences and Latin music enthusiasts. "Tito was incredibly good," remembered Pagani later. "He had a fresh sound with a jazz influence. For weeks thereafter his name kept popping up . . . dancers wanted to hear more of his music."[55] Within months, Puente's band had become so popular that he left Pupi Campo's band. At the same time, he took several other Campo band members with him. The Tito Puente band included trumpeters Frisaura and Gonzalez, pianist Varona, singer Rosa, bassist Patot, Manny Oquendo on bongos, and Frankie Colon on conga. Puente, of course, commanded the timbales, drum set, and vibraphone. Despite this talented collection of Latin performers, Puente's band "primarily performed arrangements of American pop instrumentals in which Colon (congas) did not play."[56]

The Latin spirit would not remain secondary for long, however. The music Tito Puente and his band were performing at the Palladium was drawing a mixed crowd, a multicultural and multiracial audience. "For the first time, Latinos and blacks were coming downtown to listen and dance to the exciting new sound of mambo."[57] The music these minorities were accustomed to hearing in clubs in their own neighborhoods in Spanish Harlem was now being performed in lower Manhattan. Previously, Latin music had been performed in two separate venues and styles. One was always in El Barrio for Latino fans. The other was a different sound tailored for white audiences in downtown New York. For the first time, Latin music was transcending place and audience. The Palladium was playing an essential role in that transformation:

> By the turn of the decade (1950), the Palladium Ballroom had become one of the most important Latin dance clubs in New York City. Even though the Park Palace dance hall on 110th Street and 5th Avenue could still boast about major Latin bands playing on its premises, the Palladium, situated on Broadway, began taking on the form of a Latin dance institution.[58]

The Palladium became such an important venue for Latin innovation and heavy mambo beats that it began attracting whites in droves. Everyone converged on the Palladium on Wednesday nights. That was the night Puente and his band performed. People who wanted to learn how to dance the mambo were given lessons. Crowds of spectators, music enthusiasts, and dance fans gathered in the dance studios. The audience included Latinos, blacks, Italians, Irish, Jews, and everybody in between. The audience often included movie stars, artists, and performers, all eager to hear the sounds whose reputations were making the rounds from one end of Manhattan to the other. Curious celebrities included black singer-dancer, Sammy Davis, Jr; the expressionistic artist, Jackson Pollack; actresses Marlene Dietrich and Kim Novak; and the beat poet, Allen Ginsberg. Actor Marlon Brando could be seen from time to time onstage, informally playing the bongos.

Tito Puente was becoming so sought after that he soon formed an actual, full-time band of his own. That band performed together for the first time on Independence Day, 1949, not at the Palladium, but at the El Patio Club in Atlantic Beach, New Jersey. The band's gig at the El Patio lasted for two months. Puente's group that summer consisted of seven members, but after the El Patio gig ended, he added two new players, Tony Di Risi, as the group's third trumpeter and Chino Pozo on bongos. During Puente's stint at the New Jersey club, he did some arranging for fellow bandleader, Tito Rodriguez, whom Puente had known since he was a kid. Rodriguez had Puente arrange several songs for him, which he recorded in

The Palladium was a favorite hangout for celebrities, such as Sammy Davis Jr., shown here playing the bongos at the theater in 1956. Davis was one of America's most versatile performers. He sang, danced, played several musical instruments, acted, performed comedy, and was an impressionist.

late August at the Spanish Music Center Studio. The songs included "Un Yeremico," "Frisao con Gusto," "Guarare," and "Mango del Monte."

PUENTE'S FIRST HIT

By September 1949, Puente was still making changes in his orchestra's makeup, including hiring Cuban Vicentico Valdes as his lead vocalist. The band was performing once again at the Palladium. Through the remainder of the year, Tito and his band were making recordings arranged by Puente himself. These works were written "for four trumpets, three trombones, four saxophones, and a full rhythm section of piano, bass, timbales, congas, and bongos."[59] He used this combination of instruments to record "Un Corazon," "Solo tu y yo," and "Mambo Macoco."

Puente had a recording hit, his first ever, with his arrangement of "Abaniquito," a song he arranged without saxophones and trombones. Instead, he relied on his trumpets for his brass sounds. Tico Records advertised Puente's newly recorded tune by hiring New York disc jockey Dick "Ricardo" Sugar "to host a 15-minute program and air its recordings, [where he] played 'Abaniquito' nightly and enabled Puente and Valdes to enjoy instant recognition."[60] Sales of the recording soared. Music historian Max Salazar claimed, "The people went nuts. They went looking for the band and its records, asking, 'Who is this guy Tito Puente?' That's how it started."[61] The new release was popular, not just because of Tito Puente's arranging and playing, but because "it was Valdes's fiery ad-libs and Mario Bauza's thrilling trumpet solos [that] had adrenaline flowing and enabled 'Albaniquito' to be identified with the Palladium Ballroom."[62]

Over the next couple of years, Tito Puente and his band became renowned as the foremost Latin group in New York City. Members came and went, including, in 1950, the replacement of pianist Gil Lopez with Charlie Palmieri. The

(continues on page 64)

A CIRCLE OF FRIENDS

FRIENDS, COMPANIONS, AND COLLABORATORS

During the early 1950s, Tito Puente was on his way to stardom as an arranger, performer, and bandleader of Latin music. In 1951, he released an album titled *Tito Puente and Friends*. It was, perhaps, one of the most telling titles of his career, for Tito's music was the result of his friendships, a blend of the professional and the personal, with some of the most talented of Latin and African-American musicians.

A couple of his first significant friendships with fellow musicians were with the Rodriguez brothers, Johnny and Tito. Puente and Tito Rodriguez formed a musical relationship that eventually became a friendly rivalry during the heyday of playing at the Palladium. By the early 1950s, the two Titos, along with Machito, were providing the lion's share of the most popular Latin sounds in New York City.

One of Puente's longest friendships was with an early musical influence, Jose Curbelo, whom Puente began playing alongside as early as the 1940s. He and Curbelo performed together as drummer and pianist respectively. Curbelo had a profound impact and influence on Puente during the 1940s, as Jose was destined to become one of the most famous Cuban orchestra leaders of that era. Their professional friendship helped them bring the dual Latin influences of Cuban and Puerto Rican music into a single sound.

It was under the tutelage of Jose Curbelo that Tito made another musical friend. This was the talented Cuban musician Frank Grillo, whom fans referred to as Machito. Puente first met Machito when he was 13 or 14 years old, and the Cuban became another significant model for Tito and his Latin sounds. By 1941, Puente was playing drums in Machito's band. From his friend Machito, Puente learned new aspects of music and style. Encouraged by this mentor-friend, Tito began playing the saxophone and the piano. The influences of Machito and Curbelo on Tito Puente proved to be some of the most significant in the Puerto Rican's career. Their careers paralleled across the decades, and Puente and Machito still performed together as late as the 1970s.

Another musician included in Puente's circle of friends was Noro Morales, whom Puente drummed for during those formative years of the early 1940s. It was under Morales's direction that Puente made some of his first recordings as a member of Morales's orchestra as well as his first appearances in Hollywood short films.

There were others that Puente counted as his friends and fellow musicians, including Pupi Campo. While working with Campo's orchestra in the late 1940s, Puente made another friendship, with fellow musician Jose "Joe Loco" Esteves Jr. There was Jimmy Frisaura, with whom Puente would share a friendship that lasted 40 years. Frisaura and Puente were not only close friends, but Jimmy performed in Tito's various bands, serving as his contractor. They continued to record together into the 1980s. Of course, the friendship between Puente and Mario Bauza spanned the decades as well.

Puente's longtime friendships were not always with the musicians he played with. One such exception was George Goldner, the founder of Tico Records. Goldner and Puente shared a recording relationship that extended across decades beginning in the late 1940s and stretching into the 1960s. Their friendship became so solid and professional that Puente could suggest material for an album, and Goldner would bring him into the studio the next day to cut a recording.

At times, it may have seemed like an Old Boys' Club, but musical friends also included females, especially his singers such as Celia Cruz, a Cuban-born vocalist who sang for Puente's band for years.

Music always remained the centerpiece of Tito Puente's life. The sounds and rhythms of his Latin compositions provided him with a drive and direction that gave his life meaning and purpose. Yet, music was never a solitary experience for Tito Puente the bandleader or the musician. Since he performed his music along with other musicians, he was never alone with his songs. For Puente, his fellow musicians typically became his friends and companions, some of them remaining alongside him throughout the decades of his long musical career. Puente's circle of friends was formed around sharing the songs and performances that made his career the stuff of legend.

(continued from page 61)
following year, conga player Frankie Colon was replaced by Mongo Santamaria. During the early 1950s, Puente was so popular that a rivalry developed between the Titos, Puente and Rodriguez, and their bands. The rivalry was generally friendly, since the duel between the two Puerto Rican-led orchestras only managed to generate even more interest in Latin music.

It was a great time for all Latin bands in New York City. Other bands were caught up in the fiery enthusiasm that was sweeping dance clubs and nightclubs across the city and the country. Mambo was king.

> By 1950, Tito was churning out 78s [records that played on a turntable at the speed of 78 rounds per minute, or rpms] for Tico, RCA, SMC, and Verne under names like Tito Puente y Los Diablos del mambo, Tito Puente and his Conjunto, and Tito Puente and his Mambo Boys. Mambo was the rage, and it had developed two distinct factions; the more commercially palatable sounds represented by Xavier Cugat Orchestra and Perez Praco, and the hybrid Afro-Cuban jazz sound of the Machito Orchestra, Tito Puente, and later Tito Rodriguez.[63]

Mambo had come to roost in New York City. Puente was making his career by redefining Latin music, especially his arrangements for the mambo. Yet, even as successful as he was becoming, he knew that he was not the first to take Latin jazz to new places. He had developed a style, using such Latin musicians as Machito, Mario Bauza, and Rene Hernandez, who was a pianist-arranger, as his models and inspirations. He had been there, as a younger performer, when Machito first broke ground with his new sound. In a later interview, Puente noted, "The Machito Orchestra was way ahead of its time, combining jazz and Latin. I wanted to keep that going."[64] As the sound reached the 1950s, it was Puente who was already inheriting the mantle of leadership

The mambo, the popular dance craze that swept across the United States in the 1950s, had its early origins in Cuba. New York City was home to the best mambo bands in the country, and people packed the dance halls to enjoy the pulsating rhythms of bands such as Tito Puente's.

in the further development of Afro-Cuban jazz. He was performing to large crowds of enthusiastic fans and recording constantly. Everything was coming together for the Puerto Rican band master. His sound could be heard on the radio, where "Tito Puente conquered New York with 'Babarabatiri,' 'Carl Miller Mambo,' 'Ran Kan Kan,' 'Mambo Inn,' 'Mambo City,' and 'Esy'."[65]

5

Puente, the 1950s, and Mambo

Latin music was poised to experience its highest level of commercial and popular success for the century between 1950 and 1955. That golden era would stand the music industry on its ear. Even as Puente was an important piece in the jigsaw puzzle of innovative music arrangers and leaders of his time, that era was witnessing a significant change in the course of Latin music. That major redirection was embodied in the dance rhythms of the mambo. The era would not last forever, though. By the latter years of the decade, Latin music had become so popular and practiced by even bands that were not true Latin performers, that its popularity was reached "at a cost of a dilution . . . which contributed to its decline as a nationally popular style."[66] That was a problem for another time, however. For the moment, mambo was king, and the king of mambo was Tito Puente.

DRIVING THE MAMBO

Puente was not the only driving force behind mambo and the popularity of Latin music during the early 1950s. Bandleader Perez Prado was "perhaps the first to reach large non-Latin audiences."[67] Unlike many influential Latin musicians of the mid-twentieth century, Prado did not make his reputation by performing in New York City. He was born in Cuba in 1916 and studied classical piano at Principal School of Matanzas, his hometown. He performed in local halls and dance clubs. By the late 1930s, he moved to Cuba's hottest Latin music center, Havana. In 1940, he made his first recording with the Orquesta Casino de la Playa. During those same years, he performed with other bands, including the Orquesta Cubaney and the CMQ Radio Band. By 1946, Prado was leading his own band and busy writing and arranging mambo pieces for his orchestra. Two years later, he left Cuba and went to Mexico, where he toured. In 1949, he recorded his first hit, "Mambo No. 5." Other successful records followed, including "Que Rico el Mambo," which sold a whopping 4 million copies, and "Mambo Jambo." By then, Prado was becoming extremely popular in the United States, where he first performed in the spring of 1951. (According to one story, Prado was introduced to the United States music scene through bandleader Sonny Burke who first heard Prado perform on a recording while he was vacationing in Mexico. When Burke returned home, he convinced RCA Victor to release and distribute Prado's record in the United States, where his "Mambo Jambo" was a big hit.)

That year, Perez Prado's music began reaching its largest crowds of Latin and non-Latin fans. He and his band toured the West Coast in the fall, and the band's opening date in September drew an excited crowd of 2,500 into Los Angeles's Zenda Ballroom. Two weeks later, when performing in San Francisco, Prado's audience was 3,500 fans, including both Hispanic and Anglo-American listeners. When he performed in New York City that year, however, Prado was not met as

Perez Prado was born in Matanzas, Cuba. After the success of some early recordings, he came to the United States in 1951 to further build his career. Sellout crowds packed his performances, and he was on the road to great success as a bandleader and composer. Here he appears onstage *(center, in black pants)* with his orchestra in the mid-1950s.

enthusiastically. The Latin music crowd was not as prepared for Prado's "heavy brass sound and his over-simplification did not sit well with Waldorf-Astoria clientele used to Xavier Cugat, nor with a hard-core Latin public accustomed to the greater sophistication of Machito and Curbelo, Tito Puente, and Tito Rodriguez."[68]

Just as other bandleaders, including Tito Puente, were influenced by the swing and jazz music of the 1930s and 1940s, so was Prado. His style of Cuban dance music found inspiration through his appreciation for Stan Kenton's music. Prado even hired Maynard Ferguson, Kenton's lead trumpeter, to play on some of his recordings. Driven by the power of mambo, Prado reached his height of success with his mambo rhythms by 1954. Other Prado songs helped to further establish his early 1950s name as a mambo performer, including a pair of his signature numbers, "Cherry Pink" and an instrumental arrangement of "Patricia." The Cuban mambo artist remained popular even into the early 1960s, when his star began to fade as music tastes shifted into new directions. He returned to Mexico in 1970 and died nearly two decades later.

Through Prado's influences, "the groundwork [was] laid in New York during the late 1940s" for mambo to become an extremely popular music sound.[69] His approach to the mambo sound, one that was sometimes called "progressive mambo," "lay somewhere between Tito Puente and Stan Kenton."[70] Prado had his critics, especially those who thought his mambo style catered to non-Latin audiences, resulting in a watering down of the dance beat's stylistic rhythms. It was not a criticism that such New York Latin performers as Puente or Rodriguez ever fell victim to. Perhaps they were not inclined to dilute their mambo beats because they were performing in the epicenter of the mambo movement in New York, the Palladium. It was here that the great years of the mambo's U.S. popularity took place, beginning in 1952, "when the Palladium Dance Hall switched to an all-mambo policy featuring the big bands of Puente, Rodriguez, and Machito."[71]

AN IMPORTANT YEAR

The year 1954 was a watershed time for the mambo, not only in New York City, but in the United States in general. That year, a giant national tour set out across the country, scheduled to perform in more than 50 cities from coast to coast.

The tour was arranged and booked through Mercury Artists, a major U.S. booking agency. Mercury had created an entire department dedicated to launching mambo bands. The tour was called "The Mambo-Rhumba Festival," and it included such bands as Tito Puente, Pupi Campo, the Joe Loco Quintet, vocalist Miguelito Valdes, and the Phillips-Fort Dancers. The tour spread the influences of mambo further. The music style was so popular that in the December 1954 issue of *DownBeat*, the magazine's "Everybody's Dance" list of its six best recordings included nothing but mambos. So popular was mambo that the Latin bands on the tour that year were probably paid better than nearly any other touring groups in the country.

While many different Latin and non-Latin bands were playing mambo, the music's most influential names were the younger performers, including Machito, Tito Puente, and Tito Rodriguez. These three bandleaders and their orchestras remained busy, cranking out "a steady flow of pieces that, while indisputably Latin rather than Cubop, equally indisputably drew constantly and effectively from the sister discipline."[72] Of these three Latin bandmasters, Tito Puente was the one who was best equipped to lead the way.

In part, this was due to the nature of the musical instruments he was most adept at playing. He played the timbales with a serious skill that might have been unmatched by anyone. Yet, he was also a superb musician on the vibraphone. He, in fact, must be credited with bringing the vibraphone into the equation of Latin music by the late 1940s. (He first, however, applied vibes to non-Latin ballads. He introduced them to mambo numbers later.) In addition to the vibes and timbales, his contribution to the mambo craze included his skills as a music arranger. He was also constantly experimenting and reinventing himself, his sound, and his band. In 1951, he added sax and trombone sections to his smaller band, turning it into a true "big band," a move he made, perhaps, after taking a gig at Grossingers' Catskill Mountains resort hotel in upper New York State. He also brought in Manny Oquendo to kick his rhythm section up a notch. It should come as no surprise that Tito Puente's work with mambos earned him the musical nickname El Rey del Mambo, or the King of the Mambo.

HITTING THE HEIGHTS

An entire decade of Latin music, from 1951 to 1960, belonged to Tito Puente. It was a period that would be recognized in later years as his most fertile. He released his first album that year, *Tito Puente and Friends,* on the Tropical label. It was a compilation of several of his earlier 78-rpm recordings, but this time done as a 10-inch, 33 rpm record.

Puente's popularity was skyrocketing. Although he was renowned for his own percussion skills, he added two new drummers, a conga player named Mongo Santamaria and a bongoist, Willie Bobo. Years later, these two percussionists would lead their own successful bands. In fact, they only remained with Puente until 1957, when they both left his orchestra and became members of Cal Tjader's Latin jazz group. (The legacies of Santamaria and Bobo would stretch into subsequent decades. During the 1960s, their drumming basically created the Latin-jazz-funk sound that would become the jumping-off point for the 1970s disco sound.) Puente and his band stayed busy, constantly recording between 1952 and 1955. His primary recording studio, Tico Records, gave its popular musician and his performers lots of freedom to create and experiment with their music. Puente's output was amazing, as Tico released 37 singles in 1951 alone. His relationship with Tico Records executive, George Goldner, was as smooth as silk. Tito was so popular that "all he had to do was call up George Goldner and say he had something new, and Goldner would let him record it the next day."[73]

In 1955, Puente recorded one of his most important and innovative records, the daring *Puente in Percussion.* Tito stripped down his sound to its essentials, taking away the piano and the horn section. Instead, he completely relied on his percussion section and bass. The album included himself,

Mongo Santamaria was born in Havana, Cuba, and moved to New York in 1950. There, he played with the great bands of Perez Prado, Tito Puente, and others. Santamaria was an important contributor to the development of the late 1960s boogaloo era, which gave rise to disco.

Santamaria, Bobo, and Patato Valdez on drums, along with Bobby Rodriguez on bass. The record would become a significant marking post in the history of Latin music. No one had ever done this type of sound restructuring. The effect was so convincing, popular, and successful, that "albums featuring only percussion eventually became more common on commercial Latin music labels."[74] It was a gutsy, creative move for Tito Puente and one that he recalled years later with excitement:

> George Goldner, an executive at Tico, was resistant to the project at first. He couldn't see my making an album without piano and horns. I explained to him the significance of the drum in Africa; its use in religious dance rituals and communication and how the tradition was handed down to us in Latin America. He finally gave me the go ahead on the condition that we use the studio late at night to keep the cost down. We recorded everything in one or two takes and the album was very successful both from the standpoint of sales and quality drumming.[75]

In his own words, part of Puente's motivation for arranging his album almost entirely on drums was based on mimicking African religious drum sounds. One such religious drum model was the Santeria, in which Puente had become interested. The sound had strong ties with Cuban music.

A RELIGIOUS SOUND

Santeria was a form of percussion with roots in Africa and historical arms that stretched across the Atlantic to Cuba. Over the centuries, African drums had served as the chief means of intertribal communication. They were also used during tribal religious dance rituals. This sound was brought to Cuba by African slaves who were sent by ship to the Caribbean Islands to work on the sugar plantations throughout the region, during the seventeenth and eighteenth centuries.

In looking at the roots of Santeria, fans of Latin music discovered one of the important marking posts of its development: drums. When Europeans, especially the Spanish and Portuguese, arrived along the West African coast during the 1600s and 1700s, they soon learned that the native drums were a powerful means of communication. Since the newly arrived Europeans could not interpret the messages of the drums, they came to fear them. They believed the drums were being used to rally together tribes in rebellion against the invading whites. The result was that the Spanish "banned the drums and tried to convert the Africans to Christianity and assimilate them into Western culture"[76] as they tried also to colonize the tribes of West Africa.

Of course, the Africans fought against the Europeans' practice of Christianization. They had their own religions and religious ideas, which was based in Santeria. The practices of this African religion varied from tribe to tribe. The Yoruba tribe, which became known as the Lucumis when Africans were introduced to Cuba as slaves, based their Santeria on a

A PERCUSSION SECTION TO DIE FOR

Rhythm was always the driving force of Tito Puente's musicality, an element he was always reinventing and fine tuning. He used many solid percussionists in his bands, but he may have assembled the best when he brought together the sounds of bongoist Willie Bobo and conga player Mongo Santamaria in the mid-1950s. When he recorded *Puente in Percussion*, he added congero Carlos "Patato" Valdes.

When he approached Tico Records executive, George Goldner, with his idea to record an album that relied almost exclusively on drums, Goldner could not imagine such a thing. "How can you go in the studio and just play drums?" the record producer asked Puente. Tito had to sell his idea:

> It took me a long time to convince him. I was always telling him that percussion sends a message. A percussion man is saying something. I explained to him about Africa, the mother country, where they used to send messages with their drums—you know, "I got married," "Happy Birthday," "I went bankrupt, can you lend me five dollars?"—whatever. He got a big kick about my sense of humor about drumming.*

Still, George Goldner remained unconvinced that an album driven almost strictly by percussion made much sense.

set of rituals and festivals "all based on certain rhythms and drums, combined with other wood and metal sounds."[77] In his music of the mid-1950s, Tito Puente was intent on tapping into these centuries-old religious sounds and rhythms.

The release and success of *Puente in Percussion* was not the only benchmark Tito would achieve in 1955. A package of his earlier recordings, done originally as 78-rpm records, was released by RCA Records. It was sort of a "greatest hits" tribute to the earlier musicianship of Tito Puente. That year,

As Puente remembered later:

> He still didn't want to do it. He said, "What do you mean, no horns?" I said, "Yeah, no horns, no trumpets, no saxes, no piano, no nothing, just drums." I blew his mind with that. Finally, he wanted to make me happy. He said, "I'm gonna give you the studio after midnight." I said, "That's okay, after midnight."[**]

When his players gathered in the middle of the night to create their new album, the magic began. Again, Tito recalled the first session:

> That album, we all sat around and stared at each other. Mongo brought in a bottle of Havana rum. We put it right there in the center and we had a little rum and planned the breaks and the endings to use after we finished our conversation with our drums. Everybody played great and that album turned out to be a classic—*Puente In Percussion.*[***]

* Jim Payne, *Tito Puente: King of Latin Music* (New York: Hudson Music, 2000), 30.

** Ibid.

*** Ibid.

Puente left Tico Records and signed a recording contract with RCA as his exclusive album distributor. Through the years that followed, Puente and RCA produced a large catalog of records. His initial relationship with RCA, however, was not a positive one. Although the major record company was producing albums by several Latin performers and bands, RCA and Puente differed about what sounds sold records. In an interview decades later, Puente described his initial frustrations with RCA:

> At the time, RCA was pushing Perez Prado and Luis Alcarez whom they felt appealed to a wider audience because of their toned-down approach to Latin music. Here I was ready to record with new arrangements and compositions and they put me on the back burner for three months. I finally had to go up to their offices and raise hell. From that time on at RCA they called me "Little Caesar."
>
> . . . RCA didn't know what to do with Latin music and they still don't. They treated me like some small-time, local artist yet I would consistently sell records.[78]

In 1956, RCA produced two important Puente albums, *Cuban Carnival* and *Puente Goes Jazz*, which followed *Carnival* by only a few months.

A VERY SUCCESSFUL ALBUM

Cuban Carnival would become Puente's first widely successful record album. On this album, Tito made some changes in his band. He brought in Cuban conga player Candido Camero to his rhythm section. Camero was on his way to becoming one of the most important and talented players of the 1950s and 1960s. Camero was just a couple of years older than Puente, a native Cuban who started playing bongos at the age of four. While still a youth, he learned to play bass and then conquered the drums by age 14. As with all his instruments, he was self-taught. By 1940, he was playing conga and recording while still

Machito *(center)* remained a steady and influential presence in the New York City Latin music scene. Although he did not achieve the same success as a recording artist that Tito Puente would, he continued to entertain audiences around the world until his death in 1984.

in Cuba with Machito. In 1946, Camero visited the United States for the first time. Between 1947 and 1952, he was a member of the house band at the Tropicana Club in Havana, until jazz musician Dizzy Gillespie brought him to America to play in his group. Over the years that followed, Camero played for a wide variety of jazz and Latin bands, including Stan Kenton in 1954.

A pair of songs from *Carnival* became big hits for Puente. These were "Para Los Rumberos (For Dancers)" and "Que Sera mi China." (During the early 1970s, Latin guitarist Santana had a hit of his own with this song.) The song, "Elegua Chango," was another hit on the *Carnival* album. The song was named after the Cuban Santeria god of thunder, Chango. As popular as his *Carnival* album was, *Puente Goes Jazz* would be equally significant as a commercial and artistic success. *Jazz* hit a chord with the record-buying public, and sold 28,000 copies in its first two weeks of release. For the album, Puente arranged Latin variations of several contemporary jazz numbers, as well as one of his own songs. Over the decades that followed, the album would always be remembered as a "bridge between Afro-Caribbean music and jazz."[79] When some critics accused Tito of selling out his Latin roots and "crossing over" to jazz, he could not help but be amused. "Cross over?" he asked. "I'm on my way back."[80]

The sounds created by Puente and his band on his *Jazz* album would be popular in the 1950s and continue to inspire listeners decades later. When the album was re-released more than 35 years later, its music still hit all the right notes for Latin jazz enthusiasts. As one critic noted, "Reheard from a remove of some thirty-five years, the exciting big-band Cubop on the 1956 album *Puente Goes Jazz* loses none of its immediacy and incendiary shape. Little about it is staid or dated by 1992 standards."[81] Tito had found his music, and his listeners were constantly clamoring for more. Before the 1950s slipped into the 1960s, Tito Puente had recorded more than 30 albums. His career was white hot.

6

Puente's Time and Place

With each passing year of the 1950s, the music career of Tito Puente reached new heights. With his two hit records, *Cuban Carnival* and *Puente Goes Jazz*, the year 1956 brought Puente new notoriety as a songwriter, arranger, and performer. In 1957, Puente recorded another pair of albums. The follow-up album to *Puente Goes Jazz* was a record titled *Night Beat.* It was a collection of numbers that relied heavily on jazz arrangements. Among the musicians who performed on the album was trumpet player Doc Severinson, who would one day become the bandleader on late night television's *The Tonight Show with Johnny Carson.*

TITO, MONGO, AND BOBO

Puente's second 1957 album was *Top Percussion*, a return to his earlier interest in Afro-Cuban music, especially percussion sounds. The album featured "authentic Cuban rumba—

religious-based percussion with chorus and vocal improvisation, no horns or melodic instruments of any kind."[82] Among the songs on the album was a Puente original, a solo featuring Tito on the timbales, titled "Ti Mon Bo." The song was a play on words, drawing its parts through a combination of the first syllables of the album's most important musicians—Tito, Mongo, and Bobo. Many of Puente's best musicians made their contributions to the album, including Mongo Santamaria and Willie Bobo (both of whom would leave the Puente band that year), as well as Francisco Aguabella, Julito Collazo, Enrique Marti, bass player Evaristo Baro, and a trio of singers (El Viejo Machucho, Mercedita, and Collazo). The vocalists on the record broke ground "interpreting the Lucumi (based on the African tribe known as the Yoruba) praise chants of the Afro-Cuban *santeria* religious tradition."[83] For many of those who bought Puente's *Top Percussion*, the record represented their first exposure to the connections between traditional, African religious practices, and the rhythms of modern Latin music.

The year 1957 brought another form of recognition, one that would prove hard to duplicate. That year, the Cuban government honored some of its greatest living musicians. These were the performers who had helped make Cuban music popular over the previous half century. Among those recognized was Mario Bauza. It was Bauza who insisted that Tito Puente be included among the honored for "bringing people of all backgrounds together with his Cuban-influenced music."[84] For Puente, it was a great honor. Among those recognized by Cuba, Puente was the only one who was not a Cuban.

Originally, the Cuban government had not planned on recognizing Puente at all. Plans were long under way when his friends, Machito and Bauza, had been contacted. When Puente finally realized that Cuban officials planned to celebrate 50 years of its music, and he was not invited, "he was flabbergasted at what he thought was a tremendous oversight."[85] Puente later remembered how he received a belated invitation:

(continues on page 82)

In the 1950s, Puente burst onto the recording scene with a number of critically acclaimed and popular albums such as *Cuban Carnival*, *Puente Goes Jazz*, *Night Beat*, *Top Percussion*, and *Dance Mania*. Puente's recordings were innovative compositions, featuring the top Latin musicians of the day.

(continued from page 80)

> There was this place in New York that the guys used to hang out at . . . called Barraca, on Fifty-fourth. Bobby Quintero, a Cuban newspaperman . . . told me about all these Cubans going down [to Cuba]. The Cubans were having this festival—a kind of promotion. A fifty-year celebration of recordings. I told Mario Bauza, "Hey, I played," and I had just finished *Cuban Carnival.* I said . . . "How come they's going and not me? I do more than all of them." So, they called Havana.[86]

DANCE MANIA HITS THE CHARTS

The year would not end before Puente and his band recorded yet another album, even though the album was not released until the following year. It would be his greatest. Titled *Dance*

LATIN MUSIC AND ROCK 'N' ROLL

As many music historians will explain, the heyday for Latin music in the United States was probably the decades of the 1940s and 1950s. By the 1960s, the popularity of much of this musical genre had run its course and was already beginning to lose its appeal to North American audiences. Other musical styles were taking the place of Latin music in popular culture but none more so than a type of music that was coming into its own during the 1950s, the sounds of rock 'n' roll. Yet, even as the early stages of American rock 'n roll were opening, Latin music was still making its mark. Musicologists explain today that Latin music had a strong influence on the early development of this new brand of youthful music.

Some of the early songs that would be labeled as "rock 'n' roll" were created by "grafting Latin rhythmic elements onto blues and rhythm and blues material." An early example was New Orleans pianist Roy Byrd's (also known as Professor Longhair) 1950 recording of "Mardi Gras in New Orleans," which Byrd described as "a mixture of rumba, mambo, and

Mania, the album would prove to be his most commercially successful. It remained available for decades, and, by 1994, had sold over a half million copies. In 2000, when the *New York Times* compiled the most important albums of the twentieth century, *Dance Mania* made it into the top 25.

The record's title tells the story. While Tito's *Puente in Percussion* had focused on music for drum enthusiasts, *Dance Mania* was intended to get people off their seats and onto the dance floor. Music historian Max Salazar describes Tito's intention, saying, "There was no question about what Tito had done to the music. He took it light-years ahead. When *Dance Mania* came out, that's all you heard for three years."[87] Puente did all the arranging for the album and played the timbales,

calypso."* Byrd would have a direct influence on the music style of Antoine "Fats" Domino, whose "mass-popular rhythm and blues" had "a markedly Latin cast."**

Other influences were also felt along the way as rock 'n' roll came to life during the 1950s. Guitarist Bo Diddley's 1955 release, "Bo Diddley," featured a rhythm backup section that included a floor tom roll and a dominant maracas sound. When the Coasters recorded such songs as "Down in Mexico," "Searchin'," "Young Blood," and "Poison Ivy," they had a definite Latin influence, including "drumset players [who] imitated the basic conga tumbao on the drumset by playing a backbeat on '2' and the small tom on '4' . . . [rhythms] used on countless early rock 'n' roll songs."***

* **Jim Payne, *Tito Puente: King of Latin Music* (New York: Hudson Music, 2000), 61.**

** **John Storm Roberts, *The Latin Tinge: The Impact of Latin American Music on the United States* (New York: Oxford University Press, 1979), 136.**

*** **Payne, 61.**

vibraphone, and marimba. The record featured lead singer Santos Colon, who had previously been the featured singer for the Jose Curbelo band. He delivered his vocals based on a variety of Latin rhythms, such as *son montuno*, *guaguanco*, mambo, cha-cha, and bolero. On percussion, Puente included Ray Barretto, Julito Collazo, and Ray Rodriguez. (Mongo Santamaria and Willie Bobo had left in 1957, with Ray Rodriguez replacing Bobo and Barretto sliding into Mongo's seat as bongo player.) There was Ray Coen on piano, master drummer Julito Collazo, Bobby Rodriguez on bass, and Vitin Aviles, Otto Oliva, and Santos Colon taking the vocal lead, a stint that lasted for 14 years.

Puente designed *Dance Mania* to include something for nearly everyone. The album included "Cayuco," a number that would become one of *Dance Mania*'s major hits and that would remain a dance standard for decades to follow. There was a Puente song titled, "Hong Kong Mambo," with Puente playing on marimba, tearing out a beat with an Oriental melody structure. Other songs included a Ray Santos composition, "3-D Mambo," which relied only on instrumentals inspired by jazz. Puente also included "Varsity Drag Mambo," a piece arranged to squeeze a Big Band swing sound through a jazz blender, the result being a kicky number resting on a mambo rhythm.

Dance Mania struck a chord with the Latin dance crowd immediately. Everything Tito Puente did on that album worked. He understood the sounds, rhythms, and beats that put people on the floor and swinging. He knew how to bring divergent sounds such as the horn section alongside the piano. Hilton Ruiz, one of Puente's band members, recalled how "Tito's horn lines are percussive, based on the drum beats. You just add a melody and the whole band becomes a drum."[88] His drums knew their way around a jazz harmony. As Latin musician Jerry Gonzalez noted, "Puente listens to the big band as a rhythm player, and he interprets the band as a drum."[89] There could be no doubt about Puente's skill as an arranger, musician, and performer.

Puente's album output knew no bounds during the late 1950s, as he maintained a crowded and varied schedule of making records. In 1959, he produced *Tambo*, which included the Cuban flutist Alberto Soccarras, plus trumpeters Bernie Glow, Ernie Royal, and Doc Severinson. Artistically and stylistically, the record further explored the world of Afro-Cuban music themes. Then came *More Dance Mania*, followed by recordings alongside other Big Band leaders, including Count Basie, Woody Herman, Charlie Barnett, and Abbe Lane. With Herman, Puente collaborated on the record *Herman's Heat and Puente's Beat.*

EXPERIMENTS IN MUSIC

Most of Puente's releases were successes, both commercially and artistically, yet he did not rest on the music that he knew was tried and safe. An album Puente worked on in 1960 serves as a good example of how the Latin bandleader was always ready to reinvent his music. That year, the album *Revolving Bandstand* featured a "face off" involving Tito Puente's band and trombonist Buddy Morrow's band. With two bands "competing" together in the same studio, "one with a Latin rhythm section, the other with a jazz rhythm section," the result could be little more than extraordinary and even groundbreaking.[90] The result was a stunning juxtaposition of sounds. As Tito later explained, "First the jazz big band would play a tune like 'Autumn Leaves' and give it their treatment and then the Latin band would play the bridge of the tune in authentic style."[91] The album was exciting because of the differences in time between the two bands. In listening to the recording, it is not clear how the time differentials were accommodated, but the whole thing works in a mysterious way.

Yet, the experiment was too far ahead of its time, and RCA executives refused to release the album. (The record was not released until the 1970s.) It would prove to be Puente's last album with RCA, as he left the recording company by the early 1960s. Although RCA released key records for Puente during the late 1950s and early 1960s, the company's executives never seemed to understand what Puente was trying to do with his music. As record producer, and longtime publicist for Puente,

TITO PUENTE'S LEGACY

THE SPIRIT OF PERCUSSION

Many musical genres and styles are often associated with a handful of influential performers and innovators. From jazz to pop to bluegrass to opera, many people helped to establish or enhance the musical legacy of a given style. The world of Latin music is no exception. There are numerous performers, band members, orchestra leaders, and arrangers who are remembered as those whose contributions were crucial, essential, and even historic. Among those great influences on Latin music are such names as Xavier Cugat, Don Azpiazu, Mario Bauza, Machito, Noro Morales, Tito Rodriguez, and, of course, Tito Puente.

It is impossible to rank these talents according to their ultimate contributions toward Latin-American jazz. Certainly, Tito Puente holds one of the highest positions of musical rank among them all. His influential career stretched from the 1930s until his death in the 1990s. Few of his peers developed their careers to such a depth or had as lasting an influence and legacy on the sounds associated with Latin music.

Yet, what places Tito Puente's name so close to the top of the list of Latin-American performers of the twentieth century? The answer is not an easy one. Surely, Puente's primary contribution and the backbone of his musical legacy is that he redefined what it meant to create a Latin sound as a performer, an arranger, and a bandleader.

Simply, among all the other Puente-inspired impacts on Latin music was his influence on the percussion section. Prior to Tito Puente, Latin bands and orchestras treated their drum and rhythm sections as secondary. They were viewed as the musicians who set the beat while remaining in the background, usually leaving the horn section to carry the primary musical sounds. Puente changed that musical mindset. He did so by bringing the percussive sound to the front of the music: literally, by bringing his timbales, vibraphone, and the drums to the front of the stage.

Joe Conzo, would later note, "Tito recorded literally hundreds of unreleased tracks for RCA. They just never understood how great a talent they had with Tito."[92]

The result was a sound that was so dynamic that rhythm became the driving force of the song itself. No longer were the drums secondary. They led the music, and, with the timbales in the hands of Tito Puente, the beat was driven relentlessly. It was not the horns that Puente fans danced to during his long career. It was the white-hot, sweaty percussive rhythms.

Yet, to say that Tito Puente's entire legacy as a musician lies in the placement of the percussion is to make too broad a point. Tito Puente will be remembered as the musician, arranger, orchestra leader, and recording artist who brought a new legitimacy to Latin-American music, beginning in the United States. It was within the New York music scene of the 1930s and 1940s that Tito Puente took the music and gave it, along with his fellow musicians, its new rhythms. He recognized and incorporated its sources, such as its Cuban, black jazz, and even native African sounds, into the musical equation. No one brought all these influences together better than Tito Puente.

Puente literally moved the Latin sounds out of Spanish Harlem and brought them downtown on the island of Manhattan. By doing so, he introduced his music to a whole new audience. Previously, Latin music was the music of Latinos as well as blacks from Cuba to Harlem. By lifting the music out of those ethnic contexts and delivering it to white audiences, Puente's legacy and influence on Latin music and the sounds it rests on today were made.

Today, Latin music has taken on many different forms. A new generation of performers of Latin styles such as salsa continues to keep the flame of Latin music alive. And each one, in turn, takes a cue from the legacy of one of the greatest performers and creators of Latin music of the twentieth century, Tito Puente.

Puente recorded another album in 1961, and it would become a favorite of the Latin bandleader. It was originally released as *Puente in Hollywood* and later retitled *Puente Now*. The record's producer was Norman Granz, and the record label was GNP. This was only a stopover for Puente who soon found his way back to Tico Records, his old recording studio. Puente was already recognized as a great musician, not only in America and the Caribbean, but around the world. In 1962, he went on an international tour, including Japan, where he helped solidify the popularity of Latin music.

Despite these successes, Tito Puente knew that he was competing with new musical forces at the opening of the 1960s. The 1950s had been his, with his career perhaps peaking in popularity in 1957. He was still extremely popular in the early 1960s but so was Elvis Presley and the Beatles. Rock 'n' roll was cutting a wide path through the music industry, and to some, it appeared that Latin music had already experienced its heyday. Puente plowed on, however, making more records and continuing to bring the feverish beats of Latin music to an eager audience. He continued to cut important records. In the 1960s, he made several significant albums, two of which relied heavily on the vocals of a pair of talented female artists, Celia Cruz and La Lupe.

Cruz sang for Tito Puente for several years. She and Tito had met 10 years earlier in Havana, during one of Puente's visits to the island nation. The Havana-born performer was already an established singer by the 1940s. (She and Tito were only a year apart in age.) By the mid-1950s, Celia was doing it all—singing in clubs, including the prestigious Tropicana Casino in Havana; touring throughout South and Central America as well as Mexico; lending her voice to radio and television; and appearing in movies. In 1957, she made her way to New York City and performed there for the first time. She did not know then that she would soon make New York her home. The following year, Cuba fell into political turmoil. The island's dictator, Fulgencio Batista, was hated by many, and anti-Batista revolutionaries began campaigning against his government.

POLITICS AND *PACHANGA*

By 1960, the revolution was tearing Cuba apart, and Cruz decided she could not remain in her homeland any longer. (She had already been forced to give up many of her possessions in support of the Cuban Revolution.) Before year's end, she would leave Cuba for the last time, bound for Mexico City and a gig at the La Teraza Casino nightclub. Her insightful manager had purchased her a one-way ticket to Mexico. By the following year, she was booked to appear at the New York Palladium, and, by June 1962, she was appearing at Carnegie Hall along with Tito Puente and the Count Basie Orchestra. The careers of Puente and Cruz continued together for several years. She served as his main female vocalist between 1965 and 1969.

As for the Cuban Revolution, while Cruz had escaped from the political chaos, some element of Latin music would not. When the revolution, led by Fidel Castro, turned in support of Marxism, the U.S. government turned its back on Cuba. President John F. Kennedy placed an economic embargo on Cuba, cutting off much of the trade between the United States and the island nation. The embargo included a severing of ties with Cuba that included musicians and artists. (Castro closed the same nightclubs and casinos on the island that had provided stages for many Latin artists for decades.) The result was a serious step backward for Latin music and musicians. Without direct musical influence from Cuba, "American Latin bands resorted to the same music and same dances."[93]

One of the few exceptions to this trend of relying on past themes and moves was the introduction of a new Latin rhythm called the *pachanga*. It was a fast-paced dance and musical form that surfaced for a short time but did not remain popular, according to some critics, because the beat

With a career that spanned more than 50 years, Celia Cruz was one of the most popular Cuban performers of the twentieth century. In 1966, she hooked up with Tito Puente and then recorded eight albums with him for Tico Records.

required was so fast that anyone who tried to dance to it simply exhausted themselves. Puente was not an immediate fan of the pachanga. After his 1961 return to Tico Records, his old pal, record executive George Goldner, asked Tito to make an album of pachangas. Puente at first refused but finally produced the pachanga-packed album, *Pachanga con Puente*, which was "probably his most unsuccessful recording."[94]

There would be additional disappointments for Tito Puente during the 1960s. One of those concerned his old stomping ground, the New York Palladium. In 1966, the grand old dance club closed its doors. The golden era of Latin music in New York City, an era that Tito Puente defined even as it made him a Latin superstar, had come to a close.

Through these serious changes and blows against Latin music, Puente persevered. One of the ways that Puente sometimes continued to make inroads as a musician was, ironically, "outside the realm of the Latin music industry." In 1967, he "presented a concert of his own compositions at New York's Metropolitan Opera."[95] During the late 1960s, he even hosted his own television show on a Spanish-language station, a program called *El Mundo de Tito Puente.*

Puente still had many fans, young and old. He was honored in 1968 to serve as the Grand Marshall in New York's Puerto Rican Day parade, and the following year he was again recognized by his adopted city when New York's Mayor John Lindsay gave him the symbolic key to the city. The Latin performer was far from a has-been or a throwback to earlier decades who had outlived his own previously stellar career. He not only survived the 1960s with his career intact, but he carried it into the 1970s, a decade when Latin music would experience as much change as it ever would. Even in the whirlwind of redirected Latin music of yet another decade, Tito Puente proved himself a survivor.

7 The Music Continues

Even as Puente's public life was going strong during the late 1960s and early 1970s, he was experiencing significant changes in his private life. He had married his first wife, Milta Sanchez, in 1944, but their marriage had not lasted. Their union had produced a son, Ronald, born in October 1947. Ronald had musical gifts of his own, but he was never interested in pursuing a music career. By the late 1960s, Tito had met Margie Ascension at a dance. That meeting came at an important point in Puente's life, "when he wanted to come home to someone special, perhaps raise a second family."[96] They married, and that second family soon became reality. A daughter, Audrey, was born in 1970, and a second son, Tito Jr., followed in 1972.

ANOTHER DECADE OF MUSIC

The 1970s brought new directions to Tito Puente's career as one of the leading influences on Latin music. So much of the musical past that Puente had pioneered was gone. Some of the old hands who had been bandleaders, musicians, and arrangers were gone. Some of the old venues, such as the Palladium, were no longer in operation. The fans, those enthusiasts of a straight-forward, Latin music that whirled around the dance floor, had grown up. So had the music itself. Rock music, especially, brought such dramatic changes to Latin music. In some cases, rock's influences fractured much of the legacy of earlier versions of the Afro-Cuban beat. Experimentation was the order of the 1970s, as musicians blended or even bent Latin music into new forms, creating "various combinations of blues, rock, soul, jazz, and Latin concepts."[97] The result was a collection of sounds that went beyond earlier Latin music, beyond New York City or Havana.

The 1970s was also a decade in which new artists were replacing many of the older ones. A new breed of musicians, such as Eddie Palmieri, Johnny Pacheco, Ray Barretto, and Willie Colon, were beginning to set the pace and direction of Latin music. These artists designed their own music, creating a Latin-styled form known as salsa. As with earlier Latin forms, "salsa basically adheres to the traditional structure and instrumentation of Afro-Cuban dance forms, but with significant embellishments, adaptations, and new formats and influences."[98]

Tito Puente did not believe that the music a new generation was calling "salsa" was different enough from the mambo beats he had been pounding out for decades to justify being called a new sound.

> "There's no salsa music," he said more than once during the decade. "They just put that word to the music that we were doing all the time. The mambo, the cha cha, they called it 'salsa.' You eat salsa. You don't listen to it, you don't dance to it. But the word became so popular that people ask me, 'Tito, could you play me a salsa?' So I say, 'Do you have a headache? I'll give you an Alka-Seltzer.' They gave that name to the music

(continues on page 95)

Guitarist Carlos Santana recorded Puente's song, "Oye Como Va," for his band's second album, *Abraxas*, in 1970. For over 30 years, Santana has been in the spotlight, delivering his hot brand of Latin sounds to the worlds of rock, jazz, and rhythm and blues music.

(continued from page 93)

> to give it heat, making it exciting. It's easy for everybody to say. In my concerts I always tell everybody, 'Now, we're gonna play for you—SALSA!' The audience goes, 'OHHH!' It's the same mambo I've been playing for forty years."[99]

Despite the influences that changed the direction of Latin music during the 1970s, Tito Puente was not yet resting on his past successes. In 1972, Puente released *Para Los Rumberos*, which revealed how he had lost none of his energy or vitality as a Latin musician, even as he was approaching 50 years of age. The record was a bit nostalgic, crowded with musical references to 1940s swing. Perhaps, most revealing was the title of the record's most jazz-heavy number, one that included "a gorgeous rolling baritone sax solo and give 'em-hell brass voicing. Puente had titled the song "Palladium Days."[100] Tito never stopped performing. He and his old musical comrade Machito were playing in the 1970s, putting on early evening Saturday and Sunday programs at the Corso on East 86th Street "for the aging but loyal fans—Latino and non-Latino—known to younger musicians as the "mamboniks" or "Palladium holdovers."[101]

MUSIC OF ANOTHER TIME

Even as Tito continued playing and recording, he knew that he had passed his prime by the 1970s. By 1973, he turned 50, and a younger generation of music fans considered him a great musician of a bygone era. Yet, he could still play, and he could still draw in crowds. During the late 1970s, a music critic for New York's *Village Voice* referred to Puente realistically, yet with respect, calling Puente "the Muhammed Ali of Latin music, complete with shuffle and rope a dope. After forty years, when faced with a challenge, the old man can still put it all together."[102] Although the critic was writing a review of a recent Puente concert, he had still used the term "old man." Yet, Puente defied such labels, continuing to perform not only through the 1970s but even into the 1990s.

Puente gained new audiences in the late 1970s. It was during that time that the Latin musician performed in a concert with Santana, a popular rock band, named after the group's lead guitarist, Carlos Santana. It was a melding of two different generations of Latin music (Santana was an American-born Mexican whose music combined rock, rhythm and blues, and Latin influences.) During the early 1970s, Santana had recorded two of Puente's songs, "Oye Como Va" and "Pa' Los Rumberos." Both became hits for the California band and helped boost Puente's legacy. The Santana-Puente concert, held in the Roseland Ballroom in New York, helped revitalize Puente's career, putting him into greater demand. In 1979, he was invited to perform at the White House for President Jimmy Carter.

Puente's career received another boost during the late 1970s when he was tapped by music producer Martin Cohen to participate in an international tour of great Latin musicians. Cohen was the founder of Latin Percussion, Inc., the number one manufacturer of Latin percussion instruments. To advertise his company, Cohen organized a group of Latin musicians to take his percussion instruments and their talents on the road, across Europe. When Cohen handpicked his musicians, he included Tito, whom he had heard years earlier at the Palladium. In an interview, Cohen described how it all came together:

> I signed up Johnny Rodriguez, who plays bongo with Tito and he got Tito involved. Carlos "Patato" Valdez played conga and pianist Eddie Martinez and bassist Sal Cuevas rounded out the quintet. I was thrilled to have Tito involved in the project. He made a major impact on me dating from the time I first saw him perform at the Palladium back in the early sixties. It wasn't until a few year later that I got to know Tito on a personal level. . . . By this time Latin Percussion was in its infancy and I used a set of Tito's Cuban-made timbales and timbalitos as a basis for the prototype of my ribbed-shell design. I based the "Trust

the Leader" promotional campaign on Tito's supreme skills as a bandleader and musician. . . . Through all the traveling and things that can go wrong on the road, Tito remained a constant source of inspiration.[103]

HONORS AT EVERY TURN

The tour proved to be a shot in the arm for Puente and his late-in-life career. He was only in his early fifties, but he belonged to another generation of Latin performers. He and the ensemble of musicians gave many concerts and music seminars all across Europe. In 1979, they toured Japan, introducing a new generation of another culture to the elaborate beats of Latin music. By the time the tour ended, Tito Puente was, once again, a worldwide phenomenon. As Cohen noted, "It was here, I believe, that Tito realized the worldwide popularity he had achieved."[104] There would be other milestones for Puente that year. His 1978 album, *Homenaje a Beny,* won him his first Grammy Award. (In 1977, his album, *The Legend,* had been nominated for a Grammy.) The *Homenaje* was dedicated to Cuban sonero musician Beny More. Performers on the album included singer Celia Cruz, Cheo Feliciano, Santos Colon, Ismael Quintana, Adalberto Santiago, Junior Gonzalez, Hector Casanova, Nestor Sanchez, and Luigi Texidor. It was yet another in a long string of albums Puente cut with Tico Records.

Other honors followed his Grammy, including a dinner and "roast" in his honor, hosted by *Latin NY* Magazine. Many Latin musicians attended the tribute. When they received their fees from the sponsors of the roast, the musicians donated the money to establish a scholarship fund in Puente's name to support education for young, gifted musicians. This represented an even greater tribute to Puente, who later said, "The scholarship fund was a dream of mine for a long time. In the Latin community we have a lot of gifted youngsters who don't get an opportunity to develop their talent because of a lack of money. Long after I'm gone, the fund will be helping kids."[105]

(continues on page 99)

Tito Puente is all smiles after winning a Grammy Award for his 1999 album, *Mambo Birdland.* Puente won seven Grammy Awards in three different decades, capturing honors in 1978, 1983, 1985, 1990, 1999, 2000, and 2001.

(continued from page 97)
The scholarship would provide, by the mid-1990s, more than 100 scholarships to talented people so they could study music in university and conservatory programs.

Even as Puente's career reached the 1980s, he remained a popular musician. He recorded with Concord Records in San Francisco as the Tito Puente Latin Jazz Ensemble (it was later known as Tito Puente and His Latin Ensemble). He was not the only Latin artist recording then for Concord. Cal Tjader was already working for the record label and was instrumental in suggesting that Puente do the same. As soon as the group released its first Concord album, *On Broadway*, Puente's career took yet another successful turn. The 60-ish Latin star seemed timeless to his fans, old and new.

With this release, "a major Latin music bandleader who had been associated largely with dance music that produced international hits and received media exposure was making a recording and performance commitment to Latin jazz."[106] When Cal Tjader died in 1983, Puente felt that carrying on the tradition of Latin jazz had fallen on him, and, so, *On Broadway* was a mixture of new and old, including Duke Ellington's "Sophisticated Lady." His second Concord record, *El Rey*, released in 1984, included classic jazz pieces such as John Coltrane's "Giant Steps" and "Equinox" as well as the easy sounds of "Autumn Leaves." There was a new version of Puente's "Oye Como Va" and "Ran Kan Kan" (which Tito had recorded during the 1950s). Puente was churning out the albums with Concord like clockwork. His sixth was titled *Salsa Meets Jazz*. These records brought together some of the old hats of Latin music, including Jimmy Frisaura, Bobby Rodriguez, and Johnny Rodriguez. Throughout the 1980s, Puente's ensemble won a Grammy in 1985 and 1989. By the mid-1990s, he had received four Grammy Awards and eight nominations.

Approaching 70 years of age, Puente was a titan of the music industry, an old hand who had proven himself long ago and was reproving himself constantly. He received honors constantly, including being voted, in 1987, as the top percussionist in a *Downbeat* readers' poll. He was given the Eubie Award by the national Academy of Recording Arts and Sciences that same year. By then, he had been making important contributions to the music industry for more than 50 years. The great Latin musician "had so many awards and trophies that he didn't have space for more and stored them in boxes in the basement of his home in Tappan, New York."[107]

All through his life, Tito Puente had been unable to stand still, and reaching his seventies did not slow him down. He wrote the musical score for a new play, *Lovers and Keepers.* When a television tribute was produced to honor legendary bandleader Xavier Cugat, Cugat handpicked Puente to lead

CARLOS SANTANA'S TRIBUTES TO PUENTE

While the 1970s would deliver significant changes to the world of Latin music, including new dance styles, new arrangements, new versions, and a new generation of musicians, Tito Puente would not be forgotten or left behind. In fact, he sometimes provided influences and inspirations for this new upcoming cast of musicians who wanted to play their own version of Latin music. One member of this new generation of Latin musicians was the Mexican-born American guitarist, Carlos Santana.

Santana was the son of a Mexican mariachi violinist. He began to make a name for himself as a musician by the late 1960s. As he developed his music, Carlos was directly influenced by the music sounds that were flourishing around the Bay Area of San Francisco, including the blues, rhythm and blues, and traditional Latin music. In 1969, he became popular after appearing at the first Woodstock Festival. By then, he was leading the band named for its leader, Santana. Santana recorded its version of drummer Willie Bobo's "Evil Ways" on their first album, which was titled *Santana*. When Santana the Cugat Orchestra. He scored movie soundtracks, including director Woody Allen's *Radio Days* and Luis Valdez's *Zoot Suit.* In 1992, Puente appeared in the film *The Mambo Kings,* in which he played the role of a Latin bandleader performing at the Palladium. The U.S. Congress honored his life achievements with a gold medal. There were television guest spots on *The Cosby Show* (with Dizzy Gillespie), and he did the talk show circuit, appearing with Arsenio Hall, Jay Leno, David Letterman, and Regis Philbin and Kathie Lee Gifford. The Fox cartoon series *The Simpsons* featured a Puente character in an episode. By fall 1990, Tito was honored with a star on the Hollywood Walk of Fame. That evening, Puente's Latin Jazz Ensemble performed across the street at the historic Hollywood Roosevelt Hotel.

recorded its second record, *Abraxas*, in 1970, Santana honored Tito Puente by recording a version of his 1956 cha cha "Oye Como Va." (Tito first recorded the song in 1962.) It became an instant hit for the California band, climbing to number 13 on the Billboard pop charts. Latin and salsa bands across the United States and Latin America began playing the song.

The tribute could not have made Tito happier. In an interview, he said, "'Oye Como Va' is a tune known all over the world. Everybody's played that tune. And if you don't play that tune in your repertoire, that means that you're not into nothin', see!?" (Ironically, for years following the release of Santana's version of Tito's song, fans would approach Puente and ask him if he was familiar with "that Santana tune, "Oye Como Va.") Santana also honored Puente by recording another of his songs, his 1956 "Pa' Los Rumberos" on the band's third album, *Santana III*. In 1977, the two performers took the stage together and performed at New York's Roseland Ballroom.

Puente was given many honors in recognition of his musical contributions and brilliant playing. Here, he performs with his band just hours after receiving a star on the famous Hollywood Walk of Fame in August 1990.

HITTING ONE HUNDRED

Even when Puente released his one-hundredth album, *Mambo King*, in 1991, he had not considered ending his recording career. That album was a strong compilation, and Puente had designed it to be so:

> I did this album live. I had everybody come in and play at the same time—not the trumpet on Monday and the sax on Thursday [because] I'm a dancer. I must dance in the studio while the whole band is playing to see if it really works. . . . When you hear this album . . . you'll feel the beat, you'll feel

> the vibrations—because this type of music was played and recorded like I did in the old days."[108]

The following year, he recorded *Mambo of the Times*, which brought together jazz standards from Gil Fuller and Dizzy Gillespie. There was also a number by the early twentieth-century black pianist, Fats Waller. The album's liner notes were written by Bill Cosby. Throughout the 1990s, Tito Puente continued performing, recording, teaching, and making the music he loved. He performed at New York's Carnegie Hall, and, at the other end of the country, at the Hollywood Bowl. He was playing at two dozen jazz festivals annually, in foreign locales that included England, Greece, Spain, Sweden, Singapore, Russia, Japan, Australia, and his ethnic homeland, Puerto Rico. (By the end of his career, he had performed on stage as many as 10,000 times.) By the mid-90s, Puente's son, Tito, Jr., was recording his own albums with his band, the Latin Rhythm Crew, playing Latin rap. When the younger Tito recorded his first CD in 1996, the older Tito was included, even though he hated rap music.

In 1997, RMM Records released a special tribute album honoring Tito's half century as a successful musician. The double record was titled *50 Years of Swing*. By the late 1990s, Puente's discography included 118 albums, a storehouse of 450 compositions, and 2,000 of his own arrangements. By then, he had garnered 13 Grammy nominations, winning seven of them. Then, on May 31, 2000, the 77-year-old Tito played his last. He died at the University Hospital in New York, his adopted city, during open-heart surgery intended to repair a leaking heart valve.

Four days later, on a day marred by rainstorms, Puente was put to rest in a white casket at Riverside Memorial at the corner of 76th Street and Amsterdam Avenue in Manhattan. Dressed splendidly in white, he held a pair of timbale sticks in his lifeless hands. Although Puente's family had asked for a strictly Catholic ceremony, his wife, Margie, decided to include a "private Santeria ritual out of respect for Puente's deep devotion to the Afro-Cuban religion he had long embraced."[109] Outside the funeral home, Tito's fans stood in the rain waiting for an opportunity to pay their respects at the side of the deceased bandleader's casket. They had formed their line at 7:00 A.M., and the line did not stop until the chapel closed that evening.

Two days later, a funeral procession drove through Spanish Harlem. When the cars reached 110th Street and Puente's boyhood home, the procession stopped briefly, then drove on to St. Anthony's Church in upstate New York to the small town of Tappan where the King of Mambo had his home. He was buried there, surrounded by family, friends, admirers, well-wishers, and fans. Yet, even as the bandleader, the arranger, the recording artist, the timbalist, the King of Mambo had died and been buried, the legend would live on. His music would continue to inspire rhythm and dance, and the pounding drums would echo ceaselessly.

Chronology

1923	Ernest Anthony "Tito" Puente is born in New York City at Harlem Hospital on April 20.
1935	Joins a neighborhood music and dance group, Stars of the Future, with sister, Anna.
1939	Leaves high school to become a professional musician; hired by Cuban bandleader Jose Curbelo.
1941	Plays drums in Frank "Machito" Grillo's band; also plays for Noro Morales, John Rodriguez's Stork Club Orchestra, and Anselmo Sacassas's band in Chicago; records his first albums, with Vincent Lopez's Swing Orchestra.
1942	Appears in several short films featuring the Morales Orchestra; drafted into the U.S. Navy.
1942–1945	Serves on the naval aircraft carrier, *Santee*, during World War II.
1944	Marries Milta Sanchez.
1945–1947	Attends Juilliard School of Music.
1947	Hired as a member of the Pupi Campo Orchestra; first child, Ronald, is born.
1948	Makes his own first recordings with Tico Records.
1949	Becomes a full-time bandleader; has first hit record, "Abaniquito"; band begins playing at the Palladium.
1951	Releases, through Tico Records, 37 single 45 rpms.
1955	Records one of his most innovative albums, *Puente in Percussion*, using only percussion and bass.
1956	Releases two important albums, *Cuban Carnival* and *Puente Goes Jazz.*
1957	Releases *Night Beat* and *Top Percussion;* Cuban government recognizes Tito achievements; releases *Dance Mania.*

1962 Records one of his most successful songs, "Oye Como Va."

1966 New York's Palladium closes its doors.

1967 Performs his own compositions during a concert at the Metropolitan Opera in New York City.

1970 Second child, Audrey, born to him and second wife, Margie.

1972 Third child,Tito Jr., born.

1978 Wins the first of seven Grammy Awards for his album *Homenaje a Beny.*

1979 Goes on international tour with other great Latin musicians.

1923 — 1949

1923 Ernest Anthony "Tito" Puente is born in New York City at Harlem Hospital on April 20

1939–41 Leaves high school to become a professional musician; records his first albums

1942–45 Serves on the naval aircraft carrier, *Santee*, during World War II

1945–47 Attends Juilliard School of Music

1948 Makes his own first recordings with Tico Records

1949 Becomes a full-time bandleader

1980 Friends establish a scholarship fund in his name to provide fund for educating talented young musicians.

1990 Honored with a star on Hollywood's Hall of Fame.

1991 Releases one-hundredth album.

1992 Appears in the film *The Mambo Kings.*

2000 On May 31, the King of Mambo dies of heart failure while undergoing a surgical procedure.

1955 — **2000**

1955
Records innovative album, *Puente in Percussion*

1962
Records one of his most successful songs, "Oye Como Va"

1967
Performs his own compositions during a concert at the Metropolitan Opera in New York City

1979
Goes on international tour with other great Latin musicians

1991
Releases one-hundredth album

2000
Dies of heart failure

Notes

Chapter 1

1. Steven Loza, *Tito Puente and the Making of Latin Music* (Urbana, IL: University of Illinois Press, 1999), 27.
2. Ibid.
3. Ruth Glasser, *My Music Is My Flag: Puerto Rican Musicians and Their New York Communities, 1917–1940* (Berkeley: University of California Press, 1995), 94.
4. Ibid., 95.
5. Loza, 7.
6. Ibid., 28.
7. Ibid.
8. Jim Payne, *Tito Puente: King of Latin Music* (New York: Hudson Music, 2000), 11.
9. Ibid.
10. Loza, 2.
11. Ibid.
12. Bobby Sanabria, and Ben Socolov, "Tito Puente: Long Live the King." *HIP: Highlights in Percussion for the Percussion Enthusiast* 5 (Spring/Summer): 1–7, 22–23, 1990, 1–3.
13. Ibid., 1.
14. Ibid., 3.
15. Max Salazar, "Tito Puente: The Early Years." *Latin Beat* 4, no. I: 14–20, 1994, 16.
16. Loza, 28.
17. Ibid.
18. Salazar, "The Early Years," 16.
19. Sanabria, 3.

Chapter 2

20. Salazar, "The Early Years," 16.
21. Ibid.
22. Loza, 3.
23. Ibid., 4.
24. John Storm Roberts, *Latin Jazz: The First of the Fusions, 1880s to Today* (New York: Schirmer Books, 1999), 39.
25. Ibid., 40.
26. Ibid., 41.
27. Ibid., 42.
28. Loza, 4.
29. Ibid., 29.
30. Ibid.

Chapter 3

31. Sanabria, 4.
32. Ibid.
33. Glasser, 27.
34. Loza, 4.
35. Sanabria, 4.
36. Loza, 35.
37. Ibid., 5.
38. Ibid., 36.
39. Jorge Duany, "Popular Music in Puerto Rico: Toward an Anthropology of Salsa." *Latin American Music Review* 5, no. 2: 187–216, 1984, 190.
40. Ibid.
41. Loza, 23.
42. Sanabria, 5.
43. Loza, 33.
44. Ibid., 6.
45. Payne, 24.
46. Loza, p. 20.
47. Payne, p. 24.

Chapter 4

48. Loza, 7.
49. Salazar,"The Early Years," 18.
50. Ibid.
51. Payne, 21.
52. Loza, 55.
53. Payne, 22.
54. Loza, 56.
55. Salazar, "The Early Years," 18.
56. Loza, 7.
57. Sanabria, 5.
58. Vernon W. Boggs, ed. *Salsiology: Afro-Cuban Music and the Evolution of Salsa in New York City* (New York: Excelsior, 1992), 128.
59. Loza, 9.
60. Ibid.
61. Payne, 24.

62. Salazar, Max. "Vincentico Valdes: Salsa Hitman." *Latin Beat* 3, no. 5: 28–29, 1993, 29.
63. Sanabria, 6.
64. Ibid.
65. Salazar, "The Early Years," 20.

Chapter 5

66. John Storm Roberts, *The Latin Tinge: The Impact of Latin American Music on the United States* (New York: Oxford University Press, 1979), 127.
67. Ibid.
68. Ibid.
69. Ibid., 87.
70. Ibid., 128.
71. Ibid., 129.
72. Roberts, *Latin Jazz,* 88.
73. Payne, 25.
74. Loza, 12.
75. Sanabria, 22.
76. Payne, 46.
77. Ibid.
78. Sanabria, 22.
79. Gene Kalbacher, Liner notes to *Tito Puente Goes Jazz.* RCA 66/48–4 (BMG); reissue of 1956 LP, 1993.
80. Payne, 33.
81. Kalbacher.

Chapter 6

82. Ibid., 31.
83. Loza, 14.
84. Mary Olmstead, *Tito Puente* (Chicago: Raintree, 2005), 41.
85. Josephine Powell, *Tito Puente: When the Drums Are Dreaming* (Bloomington, Ind: AuthorHouse, 2007), 220.
86. Ibid.
87. Payne, 32.
88. Ibid.
89. Ibid.
90. Sanabria, 22.
91. Ibid.
92. Ibid.
93. Powell, 263.
94. Ibid.
95. Loza, 15.

Chapter 7

96. Powell, 2.
97. Loza, 16.
98. Ibid.
99. Payne, 36.
100. Roberts, *Latin Tinge,* 178.
101. Ibid., 179.
102. Sanabria, 23.
103. Ibid.
104. Ibid.
105. Ibid.
106. Loza, 19.
107. Powell, 310.
108. "Hispanic Heritage: Tito Puente," Gale Cengage Learning. Available online at *www.gale.com/free_resources/chh/bio/Puente_t.htm.*
109. Powell, 377.

Bibliography

Boggs, Vernon W. ed. *Salsiology: Afro-Cuban Music and the Evolution of Salsa in New York City.* New York: Excelsior, 1992.

Duany, Jorge. "Popular Music in Puerto Rico: Toward an Anthropology of Salsa." *Latin American Music Review* 5, no. 2: 187–216, 1984.

Echevarria, Domingo G., and Harry Sepulveda. Liner notes to Puente, *Dance Mania.* RCA, 1958.

Glasser, Ruth. *My Music Is My Flag: Puerto Rican Musicians and Their New York Communities, 1917–1940.* Berkeley: University of California Press, 1995.

Kalbacher, Gene. Liner notes to *Tito Puente Goes Jazz.* RCA 66/48-4 (BMG); reissue of 1956 LP, 1993.

Loza, Steven. *Tito Puente and the Making of Latin Music.* Urbana, Ill.: University of Illinois Press, 1999.

Powell, Josephine. *Tito Puente: When the Drums Are Dreaming.* Bloomington, Ind: AuthorHouse, 2007.

Puente, Tito. Recorded Lecture, University of California, Los Angeles, May, 1984.

Roberts, John Storm. *Latin Jazz: The First of the Fusions, 1880s to Today.* New York: Schirmer Books, 1999.

———. *The Latin Tinge: The Impact of Latin American Music on the United States.* New York: Oxford University Press, 1979.

Salazar, Max. "Vincentico Valdes: Salsa Hitman." *Latin Beat* 3, no. 5: 28–29, 1993.

———. "Tito Puente: The Early Years." *Latin Beat* 4, no. I: 14–20, 1994.

Sanabria, Bobby, and Ben Socolov. "Tito Puente" Long Live the King." *HIP: Highlights in Percussion for the Percussion Enthusiast* 5 (Spring/ Summer): 1-7, 22-23, 1990.

Smith, Arnold Jay. "Mongo Santamaria: Cuban King of Congas." *Downbeat* 44, no. 8, 1977.

Vega, Marta Moreno. *When the Spirits Dance Mambo: Growing Up Nuyorican in El Barrio.* New York: Three Rivers Press, 2004.

Yanow, Scott. *Afro-Cuban Jazz.* San Francisco: Miller Freeman Books, 2000.

Further Reading

Flanders, Julian, ed. *The Story of Music: Gospel, Blues, and Jazz.* Volume 5. Danbury, Conn.: Grolier Educational, 2001.

Martin, Marvin. *Extraordinary People in Jazz.* New York: Children's Press, 2003.

Olmstead, Mary. *Tito Puente.* Chicago: Raintree, 2005.

Payne, Jim. *Tito Puente: King of Latin Music.* New York: Hudson Music, 2000.

Vigna, Guiseppe. *Jazz and Its History.* Hauppauge, NY: Barron's Educational Series, Inc., 1999

WEB SITES

Congahead, Tito Puente Tribute
http://www.congahead.com/Musicians/Tito_Puente_Tribute/menu.html

Drummerworld
http://www.drummerworld.com/drummers/Tito_Puente.html

Gale Cengage Learning: Tito Puente
http://www.gale.com/free_resources/chh/bio/puente_t.htm

LP (site of Latin Percussion drum manufacturer)
http://www.lpmusic.com/The_LP_Family/tito_tribute/tito_index.html

The Official Site of Tito Puente, Jr.
http://www.titopuentejr.net

Picture Credits

page:

8: Associated Press
11: Associated Press
13: Associated Press
22: Frank Driggs Collection/Getty Images
27: Associated Press
31: Michael Ochs Archives/Getty Images
32: Michael Ochs Archives/Getty Images
35: Michael Ochs Archives/Getty Images
42: Frank Driggs Collection/Getty Images
45: Frank Driggs Collection/Getty Images
60: AP Photo/Marty Lederhandler
65: Yale Joel/Life Magazine/Time & Life Pictures/Getty Images
68: Frank Driggs Collection/Getty Images
72: Walter Iooss Jr/Getty Images
77: Frank Driggs Collection/Getty Images
81: Michael Ochs Archives/Getty Images
90: Michael Ochs Archives/Getty Images
94: AP Photo/Kathy Willens
98: Jeff Vespa/Wire Image
102: AP Photo/Kevork Djansezian

cover: © Photofest

Index

A

"3D Mambo" (song), 84
50 Years of Swing (album), 103
"Abaniquito" (song)
  arrangement of, 52, 56–57, 61
Academy of Recording Arts and Sciences, 100
African
  history, 74
  religious drum sounds, 73–75, 80, 87, 104
African-Americans
  music, 37, 62
  neighborhoods, 9, 18, 26
Afro-Cuban, 104
  music, 10, 12, 30, 36, 40, 51, 53, 65, 78–79, 85, 93
Afro-Cubans (band)
  formation, 36–37
Aguabella, Francisco, 80
Alcarez, Luis, 76
Allen, Woody, 101
Alma Dance Studios, 52, 54
Alvarez, Fernando, 46, 51
Amos and Andy (radio), 9
Arcadia ballroom, 54, 56
Asia
  at war, 10–12
Astaire, Fred, 23
Austria, 6
Autry, Gene, 9
Aviles, Vitin, 84
Azpiazu, Don, 34, 86

B

"Babarabatiri" (song), 65
"Bajo de Chapotin, El" (song), 44
Barnett, Charlie, 85
Baro, Evaristo, 80
Barretto, Ray, 84, 93
Barrio, El
  growing up in, 10, 17–19, 23
  music world of, 23, 26, 38, 55, 58
Bastista, Fulgencio, 88
Bauza, Mario, 12
  bands, 36–37, 41, 52–53, 63–64, 80–81
  influence of, 86
  trumpet solos, 55, 61
Beatles, 88
Bender, Richard, 49
Big Band sound
  leaders, 24, 37, 43, 84–85
Blen Blen Club, 55
Blondie (radio), 9
Bobo, Willie
  playing with, 71–72, 74, 80, 84, 100
Bob Hope Show, The (radio), 9
Bolero, 84
"Botellero, El" (song), 41
Brandt's Theatre, 36
Burke, Sonny, 67
Byrd, Roy, 82–83

C

"Cachita" (song), 39
Camero, Candido, 76–77
Campo, Pupi
  band, 47, 50–51, 54, 57–58, 63, 70
"Carl Miller Mambo" (song), 65
Carnegie Hall, 89, 103
Carter, Jimmy, 96
Casa Cubana club, 33
Cassanova, Hector, 97
Castro, Fidel, 89
Central Commercial High School, 21, 26
Cha Cha, 25, 84, 93
Charlie Spivak Orchestra, 44
Chicago Colony Club, 39
"Clair de Lune" (song), 46
Clef label, 37
Club Yumuri, 33
CMQ Radio Band, 67
Coasters, 83
Coen, Augusto, 40
Coen, Ray, 84
Cohen, Marty, 96–97
Cohito, 12
Collazo, Julito, 80, 84
Colon, Frankie, 52, 58, 64
Colon, Santos, 84, 97
Colon, Willie, 93
Coltrane, John, 99
Concord Records, 99
"Conga, La" (song), 39
Conzo, Joe, 87
Copacabana, 14
  band, 46, 51
Cosby, Bill, 103
Cosby Show, The (television), 101
Count Basie, 26, 50, 85, 89
Crosby, Bing, 13
Cruz, Celia, 63, 88–89, 97
"Cuando te Vea" (song), 50
Cuba, 9
  dance sound, 34, 37, 43
  entertainers, 27, 30–31, 67–68, 76–77, 85
  government, 80, 88–89
  music, 33–34, 36–37, 62–63, 65, 69, 73, 79–80, 87, 93
  nightspots, 36
  orchestras, 30–31, 34, 37–38
  Revolution, 89
Cuban Carnival (album), 76, 78–79, 82
Cuban Pete (film), 40
Cuevas, Sal, 96
Cugat, Xavier
  bands, 9, 12, 31, 43, 51, 64, 68, 100–101
  influence of, 86
Curbelo, Jose
  band, 32–33, 46–47, 55, 62, 68, 84
  influence of, 30–33, 37, 39, 41, 62
Czars of Harlem, 34
Czechoslovakia, 6

D

Dance Mania (album), 82–84
Dancing
  lessons, 23, 25
Davis, Sammy, Jr., 59
Decca Records, 12, 40

De La Hoya, Oscar, 31
Denmark, 7
Diddley, Bo, 83
Dietrich, Marlene, 59
Di Risi, Al, 52, 57
Di Risi, Tony, 57, 59
Disco, 71
"Dolor cobarde" (song), 27
Domino, Antoine "Fats," 83
Dudley, Bessie, 36

E
"Earl Wilson Mambo, The" (song), 50
"Eco" (song), 41
"Elegua Chango" (song), 78
Ella (film), 40
Ellington, Duke
  career, 26, 28, 37, 99
Embassy Club, 54
Escobar, Al, 57
Escolies, Tony, 40
"Esta Frizao" (arrangement), 50
Esteves, Jose, Jr. *See* Loco, Joe
Estrella Habanera, Las club, 38
"Esy" (song), 56–57, 65
Eubie Award, 100
Europe, 74
  at war, 6–7, 10–12, 41, 43

F
"Fast and Furious" (show), 36
Federico Pagani's Happy Boys
  playing with, 10
Feliciano, Cheo, 97
Ferguson, Maynard, 69
Films
  appearances in, 40, 43, 63
  soundtracks, 101
France, 7
Fred Allen Show, The (radio), 9
"Frisao con Gusto" (song), 61
Frisaura, Jimmy
  career, 47, 52, 57–58, 63, 99
Fuller, Gil, 103

G
Galindez, Polito, 32
Gay Ranchero, The (film), 40
Germany
  Nazi troops, 6–7, 9, 41
  at war, 6–7, 9, 12, 41
Gilberto Valdes orchestra, 31
Gilbert and Sullivan operettas, 14
Gillespie, Dizzy, 77, 101, 103
Ginsberg, Allen, 59
Glow, Bernie, 85
GNP records, 88
Goldman, George, 50
Goldner, George
  working with, 63, 71, 73–74, 90
Gonzalez, Chino, 54, 58
Gonzalez, Jerry, 84
Gonzalez, Junior, 97
Goodman, Benny
  orchestra, 28
Gordon, Mack, 36
Go West, Young Man (show), 12
Grammy Awards, 97, 99, 103
Granz, Norman, 88
Great Britain
  at war, 7, 41
Great Depression, 7, 9, 17, 47
Green Hornet, The (radio), 9
Grillo, Frank. *See* Machito
Grillo, Mario, 37
Grillo, Paula, 37
Grossingers' Catskill Mountains, 70
"Guarare" (song), 61

H
Happy Boys band, 55
Harlem
  music scene, 33–34, 56, 58
  neighborhoods, 9, 14, 17–19, 21, 24–26, 47, 51, 54, 87
"Harlem Rhumbola" (song), 36
Havana Casino Orchestra, 34
Havana-Madrid club, 12, 33, 47
Havana Riverside orchestra, 31
Hayworth, Rita, 43
Hermanos Lebartard orchestra, Los, 31
Herman's Heat and Puente's Beat (album), 85
Herman, Woody, 85
Hernandez, Rene, 64
Hernandez, Victoria, 23–24
"Hijos de Buda, Los" (song), 39
Hitler, Adolf
  troops, 6–7, 41
Homenaje a Beny (album), 97
"Hong Kong Mambo" (song), 84
"How High the Moon" (arrangement), 50

I
Ink Spots Quartet, 26
Italy, 41

J
Jack Benny Program, The (radio), 9
Jack Cole Dancers, 41
Japan, 88, 97
  at war, 10–14, 41
Jazz
  Afro-Cuban, 30, 36–37, 51, 53, 65
  musicians, 26, 34, 37, 49, 53, 71, 78

rhythms, 24–25, 44, 46, 53, 58, 64, 69, 79, 84–87, 95, 99
Jones Act, 19
Juilliard School of Music, 48–51

K
Kennedy, John F., 89
Kenton, Stan, 49, 69, 78
Krupa, Gene, 28

L
La Conga club, 12, 33, 47
Lafayette Theater, 34, 36
La Lupe, 88
Lane, Abbe, 85
Latin
bandleaders, 12, 23, 30–31, 34, 36–37, 39, 43, 53, 55, 58, 62, 67–70, 85–86, 88, 93, 97, 101, 104
entertainers, 23–25, 29–30, 58–59
immigrants, 9, 18, 42–43
music, 9–10, 12, 14, 20, 24–26, 30–31, 33–34, 36–41, 43, 47, 50–54, 58–59, 61–64, 66–73, 76, 78, 80–81, 84–89, 91–93, 95–97, 99–100
neighborhoods, 9, 17, 20–21, 48
pride, 24–25, 43
Latin Percussion, Inc., 96
Latin Rhythm Crew, 103
Legend, The (album), 97
Lewis, Jerry, 47
Lindsay, John, 91
Loco, Joe
career, 50–51, 54, 63, 70
Lone Ranger, The (radio), 9
Lopez, Gil, 61
Lopez, Mano, 12
Lopez, Vincent
swing orchestra, 39
Lovers and Keepers (album), 100

M
Mabley, Jackie, 37
Machín, Antonio, 34
Machito (Frank Grillo), 9, 52
death, 37
influence of, 30, 36–39, 41, 62, 86
military, 37
playing with, 12, 24, 50
orchestra, 12, 24, 36–37, 40–41, 44, 46, 51, 53, 55–56, 62, 64, 70, 77, 80, 95
Machucho, El Viejo, 80
Mambo, 104
new sound of, 55, 58–59, 69, 71, 84
popularity of, 64–71, 82, 93, 95
tour, 69–70
"Mambo City," 65
"Mambo Inn" (song), 65
"Mambo Jambo" (song), 67
Mambo King (album), 102
Mambo Kings, The (film), 101
"Mambo Macoco" (song), 61
"Mambo No. 5" (song), 67
Mambo of the Times (album), 103
Mambo-Rhumba Festival, 70
Marshall, Kaiser, 34
Marti, Enrique, 80
Marti, Frank, 46
Martin, Dean, 47
Martinez, Eddie, 96
Marxism, 89
Melody Ranch (radio), 9
Metropolitan Opera, 91
Mexican Jumping Bean, The (film), 40
Miranda, Carmen, 43
"Mis Amores" (song), 46
Montecino's Happy Boys, 51
Morales Brothers Orchestra, 40
Morales, Nino, 41
Morales, Noro, 9
influence of, 10, 39–40, 50–51, 55, 63, 86
More, Beny, 97
More Dance Mania (album), 85
Morrow, Buddy, 85
Morton, Tommy
and the Palladium, 54–56
Mullinder, Lucky, 26
Mundo de Tito Puente, El (television), 91
Murrow, Edward R., 7
Musicians Union, 29–30

N
New York City, 18
childhood in, 16–17
clubs and dance halls, 9–10, 12, 14, 33–34, 36–37, 51, 53–54, 58–59, 61–62, 64, 67–68, 93
music in, 9–12, 14, 24–26, 30–34, 38, 40, 43, 48, 50, 62, 69, 87–89, 91
New York School of Music, 23
Nieto, Uba, 46
Night Beat (album), 79
Noro Morales Orchestra
playing with, 10, 40
Novak, Kim, 59

O
Oliva, Otto, 84
On Broadway (album), 99
Oquendo, Manny, 58, 70
Orquesta Casino de la Playa, 67
"Oye Como Va" (song), 96, 99, 101
"Oye Negra" (song), 40

P
Pachanga, 89–91
Pachanga con Puente (album), 91
Pacheco, Johnny, 93

Pagani, Federico
career, 54–55, 58
Palace Theater, 34
Palladium, 37, 101
bands at, 52–55, 89
playing at, 52, 57–59, 61–62, 69, 91, 93, 96
"Palladium Days" (song), 95
Palmieri, Charlie, 57, 61, 93
"Pa Los Rumberos" (song), 96
Para Los Rumberos (album), 95
"Para Los Rumberos" (song), 78
Parker, Charlie, 37
Park Palace, 59
Patio Club, El, 59
Patot, Manuel, 54, 57–58
"Peanut Vendor, The" (song), 34
Pearl Harbor
bombing of, 13–14, 41
Percussion
paid jobs, 30, 33, 36–38, 40–41, 47, 62
studying, 10, 24–25, 28
style, 38, 41, 56–57, 63, 70, 71–75, 80, 83–84, 86–87, 100
Perla del Sur, La (club), 46
Phillips-Fort Dancers, 70
Piano
paid jobs, 38, 46, 54
studying, 10, 23–24, 27
"Picadillo" (song), 54, 56–57
"Pierdate" (arrangement), 50
"Pilarena" (song), 50
Playa, Casino De La, 27
Poland, 6, 41
Pollack, Jackson, 59
Pozo, Chino, 52, 57, 59
Prado, Perez
career, 64, 67–69, 76
Presley, Elvis, 88
Principal School of Matanzas, 67
Puente, Anna (sister)
childhood, 17, 23
death, 46
music education, 21
Puente, Antonio (grandfather), 19
Puente, Audrey (daughter), 92
Puente, Ercelia (mother)
immigration, 16, 19, 24
influence of, 21, 23
Puente, Ernesto (father)
immigration, 16, 19, 24
work, 16
Puente Goes Jazz (album), 76, 78–79
Puente in Percussion (album)
innovative sound of, 71–72, 74–76, 83
Puente, Margie Ascension (wife), 92, 103
Puente, Milta Sanchez (wife), 46, 92
Puente Now (album), 88
Puente, Robert Anthony (brother), 17
Puente, Ronald (son), 92
Puente, Tito
birth, 16–17, 19, 24
charity, 97, 99
childhood, 16–18, 20–21, 23, 26
chronology, 105–107
death, 16, 103–104
education, 21, 26, 28–29
military, 14–15, 41–44, 46, 49
music education, 10, 21, 23–24, 26–29, 48–50
religion, 22
Puente, Tito, Jr. (son), 92, 103
Puerto Rico
entertainers, 24–25
heritage, 16, 20, 24, 91
immigrants, 9–10, 16, 18–20, 24, 30, 46, 48
language, 20–21
music, 33–34, 40, 62–65
neighborhoods, 17–19

Q
"Que Rico el Mambo" (song), 67
"Que Sera mi China" (song), 78
Quintana, Ismael, 97
Quintero, Bobby, 82

R
Radio Days (film), 101
"Ran Kan Kan" (song), 65
RCA Victor Records
albums with, 34, 64, 75–76, 85–87
Rector, Eddie, 36
Revel, Harry, 36
Revolving Bandstand (album), 85
Rey, El (album), 99
"Rhapsody in Black" show, 36
"Rhumba-Land" (show), 34
"Rhumbatism" (song), 36–37
RMM Records, 103
Rock 'N' Roll, 88
Latin music influence on, 82–83, 93, 96
Rodriquez, Bobby, 72, 84, 99
Rodriguez, Johnny
career, 30, 39–40, 62, 96, 99
Rodriguez, Pablo "Tito"
career, 9, 30, 33, 40, 51, 53, 59, 62, 64, 68–70
influence of, 86
Rodriquez, Ray, 84
Rosa, Angel, 57–58
Rogers, Ginger, 23
Roseland ballroom, 54, 56, 96, 101
Royal, Ernie, 85
Royal Havana Troupe, 34
Ruiz, Hilton, 84
Rumba, 25, 33, 79
bands, 34, 43, 55, 82

S
Sacassas, Anselmo
band, 27, 39–40
Salazar, Max, 56, 61, 83
Salsa, 87, 93, 95
Salsa Meets Jazz (album), 99
Sambas, 25
Sanabria, Juancito, 31
Sanchez, Nestor, 97
San Juan, Olga, 23
Santamaria, Mongo
playing with, 64, 71–72, 74–75, 80, 84
Santana, 78, 96
albums, 100–101
Santana, Carlos, 96, 100–101
Santeria
influence of, 73–75, 104
Santiago, Adalberto, 97
Santos, Ray, 84
Saxophone, 44, 95
lessons, 23
paid jobs, 38
Schillinger, Joseph, 49
Schillinger System of Music, 49–50
Severinson, Doc, 79, 85
Shaw, Artie, 28
Simpsons, The (television), 101
"Sing, Sing, Sing" (song), 28
SMC records, 64
Smith, Mamie, 34
Soccarras, Alberto, 85
"Solo tu y yo" (song), 61
"Son de la Loma" (arrangement), 50
Soviet Union, 12
Spain, 19, 73
Spanish-American War, 16, 19
Spanish Music Center Studio, 61
Stars of the Future, 21, 23
Stork Club, 10
orchestra, 39
Sugar, Dick "Ricardo," 61

T
Tambo (album), 85
Tango, 43
Tarzan (radio), 9
Texidor, Luigi, 97
Tico Records
albums with, 50, 61, 64, 71, 73–74, 76, 88, 90
"Ti Mon Bo" (song), 80
Tito Puente and Friends (album), 62, 71
Tito Puente Latin Jazz Ensemble, 99
Tito Puente and the Picadilly Boys, 57
Tjader, Cal, 71, 99
Tonight Show with Johnny Carson, The (television), 79
Top Percussion (album), 79–80
Tropical records, 71
Tropicana Casino, 88
Tropicana Club, 77

U
"Un Corazon" (song), 61
United States, 6
citizenship, 18–19, 24
economy, 7, 9, 17, 47–48
government, 12, 18–19, 89
military, 19, 41–44, 47, 51
music, 9
radio, 9
at war, 13–15, 17, 19, 41–44, 46, 49
"Un Yeremico" (song), 61

V
Valdes, Miguelito, 54, 70
Valdes, Vincentico, 52, 61
Valdez, Luis, 101
Valdez, Patato, 72, 96
Varona, Luis
career, 24, 52, 57–58
"Varsity Drag Mambo" (song), 84
Verne records, 64
Vibraphone
playing, 49–50, 58, 70, 86

W
Waldorf-Astoria, 68
Waller, Fats, 103
Water, Ethel, 36
Webb, Chick, 26
World War I, 18–19, 41, 48
World War II, 49
events of, 6–7, 9–15, 41–44, 46, 48
WOR studios, 51
Writing music
learning, 44, 46, 49–50
style, 56–57, 79

Y
"Yumba" (song), 39

Z
Zenda Ballroom, 67K

About the Author

TIM McNEESE is an associate professor of history at York College in York, Nebraska, where he is in his sixteenth year of college instruction. Professor McNeese earned an associate of arts degree from York College, a bachelor of arts in history and political science from Harding University, and a master of arts in history from Missouri State University. A prolific author of books for elementary, middle and high school, and college readers, McNeese has published more than 90 books and educational materials over the past 20 years, on everything from Spanish painters to American political movements. His writing has earned him a citation in the library reference work, *Contemporary Authors.* In 2006, Tim appeared on the History Channel program, *Risk Takers, History Makers: John Wesley Powell and the Grand Canyon.* He was a faculty member at the 2006 Tony Hillerman Mystery Writers Conference in Albuquerque, where he presented on the topic of American Indians of the Southwest. His wife, Beverly is an assistant professor of English at York College. They have two married children, Noah and Summer, and two grandchildren, Ethan and Adrianna. Tim and Bev sponsored study trips for college students on the Lewis and Clark Trail in 2003 and 2005 and the American Southwest in 2008. Readers may contact Professor McNeese at tdmcneese@york.edu.